AFTER HOURS

AFTER HOURS

CLAIRE KENNEDY

Simon Pulse

New York   London   Toronto   Sydney   New Delhi

SIMON PULSE

An imprint of Simon & Schuster Children's Publishing Division

1230 Avenue of the Americas, New York, New York 10020

This Simon Pulse edition June 2015

Text copyright © 2015 by Simon & Schuster, Inc.

Cover photographs copyright © 2015 by Thinkstock

All rights reserved, including the right of reproduction in whole or in part in any form.

SIMON PULSE and colophon are registered trademarks of Simon & Schuster, Inc.

For information about special discounts for bulk purchases, please contact

Simon & Schuster Special Sales at 1-866-506-1949 or business@simonandschuster.com.

The Simon & Schuster Speakers Bureau can bring authors to your live event. For more information or to book an event contact the Simon & Schuster Speakers Bureau at 1-866-248-3049 or visit our website at www.simonspeakers.com.

Cover designed by Russell Gordon

Interior designed by Bob Steimle

The text of this book was set in Palatino LT Std.

Manufactured in the United States of America

2 4 6 8 10 9 7 5 3 1

Library of Congress Cataloging-in-Publication Data

Kennedy, Claire.

After hours / Claire Kennedy.—Simon Pulse edition.

pages cm

Summary: "Scandals and hook-ups abound in a summertime restaurant drama where four teens are all willing to do whatever it takes to make it through the work day . . . and hopefully to win the money in the afterhours dare-based game of Tips."—Provided by publisher.

[1. Conduct of life—Fiction. 2. Secrets—Fiction. 3. Restaurants—Fiction. 4. Summer employment—Fiction.] I. Title.

PZ7.1.K5Af 2015

[Fic]—dc23

2014026914

ISBN 978-1-4814-3016-6 (hc)

ISBN 978-1-4814-3015-9 (pbk)

ISBN 978-1-4814-3017-3 (eBook)

For my parents

AFTER HOURS

Isa
Wednesday

"It's the rules," Finn says. "New kids have to wait on the Witch at table twelve." He grins at me, and his eyes go all crinkly. He probably thinks he's adorable, all muscles and short blond hair, but he doesn't work on me. I know his kind. He's being weird and condescending to get me to like him. He's trying to rattle me.

"No problem, Finny," I say, sugary sweet. It's my third lunch shift, after all. I've got this. I waltz out into the restaurant with my pen whipped out and a perfect, professional smile plastered all over my face. For breakfast, lunch, and early dinners, people come to Waterside Café for excellent service and divine food made by a world-renowned chef who was recently featured in *Food Weekly*. But after five p.m., people come to Waterside Café for the food, the service, and, most importantly, to order too many cocktails.

As for the Witch at table twelve—I heard about her five days ago, when I started. She's infamous, and apparently a megafreak. She hits on the male waiters and is unfailingly cruel to the girls. I heard she told Xavi, this busgirl who always gets the late shift, that her wig looked like burnt plastic. Except Xavi doesn't wear a wig.

I take a slow, deep breath, pull my pad of paper out of my cummerbund, and—holy shit.

I recognize the woman—the Witch at table twelve.

I don't just recognize her. I *know* her.

Katerina Roland.

I have to go back to the kitchen. I have to tell Finn that, I don't know, she tried to scratch me with her ugly press-on nails or mace me with her bottle of overly floral perfume.

But she sees me. And she waves me over with two flicks of her gold-bangled wrist.

Maybe she won't recognize me. Usually when I'm around her I look . . . different.

"Can I help you?" I ask, trying to sound bright and cheerful.

"Uh," she says, "can you?" She pulls down her bright red glasses and peers at me.

Great. She's going to be one of those. Still, she doesn't recognize me. I don't think. I'd rather be anonymous waiter girl than—myself. Or whoever she thinks I am.

"Have you had a chance to look at the menu?" I say. I will not be daunted. She loves me, after all. Well, usually.

She looks at me closely. Does she recognize me without all the makeup? I hope not. Otherwise, being the newest waitress at Waterside is going to be a lot less fun.

"Honey." Her voice drips with condescension. "*Honey.* I'm what those in the restaurant world call a *regular*. I know this menu better than you. I'll take a cheese plate. I want extra rice crackers, two thin slices of tomato, and three slices

2

of cucumber. I want the Niçoise salad, but tell that fool cook of yours I'll strangle him if he tries to put salmon on it again. I need a new water with four ice cubes. This one," she points at her glass, which already has garish lipstick marks all over the rim, "has *seven*." She drums her fingers on the white tablecloth.

I make a few cursory marks on my notepad. "Anything else?"

Mrs. Roland sniffs at me. "You can go."

I resist the urge to make a snarky remark. I turn away, but as I do, I hear her:

"Wait."

I stop, but I don't turn around. She knows. I know that she knows.

"You're Isabel Sanchez, aren't you?"

I turn back to her. Damn it. I look left and right. None of the other waitstaff are around, and Rico, who owns the place, has disappeared from his post at the bar.

"Yeah," I say. "Hi, Mrs. Roland."

Her whole face lights up like a glow worm. "Oh, Isabel! You look so different without your makeup! So fresh! What are you doing here, darling? Don't you make enough money winning pageants?"

And there it is. My deep, dark secret.

I, Isa Sanchez, could have starred on *Toddlers & Tiaras*. I have been in rhinestones since before I got out of diapers.

I'm a pageant queen.

And I hate every freaking second of it.

Still, a girl has to have money. Especially me.

"College will be expensive, Mrs. Roland."

She winks at me, and her false eyelashes shift. "Sure," she says. "College."

I give her my best pageant smile, but we both know I'm not saving for college. When I don't win cash for parading across a stage in a bikini, I at least get a nice untouchable scholarship put away for me. I've got enough for four years at any college. God knows I'd prefer cash with the way I live now—if you call living in a double-wide with my great-aunt "living."

"How are your parents?" she asks. "Doing well out on the road?"

"Brilliantly," I answer, with my smile fixed in place. It's a complete lie, but it's one I'm used to telling. It's gotten easier with time.

"Mmm," she says, and takes a sip from her water and grimaces.

Why do I feel like I'm naked in the interview portion of a pageant right now? "May I get anything else for you, Mrs. Roland?"

She flaps her wrists around. "Candles," she says. "I need atmosphere, darling, and this place simply doesn't have enough for me."

Candles. At lunchtime.

Whatever.

Finn
Wednesday

I watch Isa waiting on the Witch and try not to snicker.
Last time a new girl waited on the Witch, she quit. Just ditched
her stuff and booked it. She didn't even come back for her paycheck, which would only be, like, twelve bucks anyway. Ever
since, Rico's been all about using the Witch—Mrs. Roland, who
I guess married rich—as a test case. If the waitstaff can't handle
her, he doesn't want them. He only wants the best waitstaff
for his restaurant, seeing as how it's competing with General
Steakhouse, a ritzy Texas-style joint, since last year.

Isa returns to the kitchen, tears the top sheet off her pad,
and hangs it in front of Peter, the cook. Peter's the man.
Everybody likes Peter.

"You survived," I say. "Nice."

She shoots me a look. "You're surprised? She was about
as mean as you are smart." She tosses her long brown hair at
me, in the way that girls do that means they're a little pissed
but also sort of trying to show off. She's pretty. Kind of. I
think. Maybe in a classic way or something. I don't know.

"You should wear jewelry," I say. "Earrings and a pearl
necklace, I think. To be, like, fancier."

Now she gives me an evil look, like she wants to scratch my eyes out. "Excuse me, you jock asshole? A pearl necklace?"

Oh shit. "I didn't—"

"Screw. You." She spits the words at me, turns on a heel, and stalks out toward the dining room. But before she reaches the threshold, she pauses and straightens her posture. Hmmm. Professional. Not bad. Rico'll be happy, at least.

Behind the stove, Peter starts laughing.

"What?" I ask, but I get it.

"You're sick, man," he says. "Propositioning the new girl on your first training shift with her? Nice."

I laugh too. Better to sound like an asshole than an idiot. "Yeah, man. I didn't think she'd get it."

Peter shakes his head, and some of his black hair comes loose from the hairnet. "No wonder you don't get chicks, dude. A good-looking guy like you? All-state football and wrestling? You got it made, man. And then you open your mouth and ruin it all."

I resist the urge to protest. Peter doesn't know.

"And you get girls? I think you're all talk," I say instead.

Peter just grins at me in this stupid, irritating way, because he doesn't talk much about girls at all. He doesn't need to. He just looks at girls with his floppy hair in his dark eyes and their clothes just disintegrate off their bodies. It's fucking magical.

"Shot?" he asks. He pulls out a bottle of bourbon. Expensive bourbon, used only for cooking tonight's special—a bourbon rib-eye steak. Famous in three states. Let General Steakhouse try to top that.

"Yeah," I say. He pours out a couple and we take them,

wincing at the burn. Even good bourbon isn't as smooth as everyone says it is.

"Pour me one," Isa says from behind us. She grabs a drying shot glass from the open industrial dishwasher and slams it on the table. "Now."

Peter tips the bourbon bottle and pours her a full one, and she downs it without blinking.

"Damn, girl," Peter says. "Respect."

"Respect," I echo.

She glares at me and wipes her mouth off on the back of her wrist. "Whatever. I need to get candles for Mrs. Roland's table. She wants ambiance or something."

"They're in the closet by the fridge," Peter advises.

"Thanks." She flashes him a smile—a real one—and I actually feel a little bad. She swipes a couple of candles from the closet and a lighter from Peter's back pocket. He grins at her.

"She's not bad," he says, watching her walk away. "Think we should let her in the game, man?"

"Not yet," I say. "I don't trust her."

Peter takes a pass of the bourbon, straight from the bottle. "I don't know, man. I think she's perfect. I mean, yeah, maybe we can give her a few more days. But if Xavi says yes and Rico likes her, I say she's in."

"Why Xavi? I mean, I know she's your stepsister, but she's a busgirl. She's hardly ever even able to buy in."

Peter gives me a sharp look. "She's a good judge of character."

"What if Isa doesn't want to be in?"

Peter shakes his head. "Finn, everyone wants to be in. Everyone."

7

He's right. No one turns down Tips.

"I'll talk to Rico," he says. He pours himself a little more bourbon. Peter can drink like a madman and still come off like Tom Brady.

"I don't know, man," I say. "There's something off about her. I haven't decided yet."

Peter walks around the kitchen to the refrigerators and cuffs me on the arm. "There's something off about you, too, dude. But we still let you play."

I reach across and down his bourbon. Peter has no idea how right he is.

Xavi
Thursday

I'm going to win. I have to.

I fix my hair and reapply my lipstick, using the stainless-steel refrigerator as a mirror. A job at Waterside requires perfection on the floor if you want to keep your job, and if there's no job, there's no game. Annoyingly, the game's probably off for this weekend. It's off whenever a new person is hired. We can't take any chances until Rico gives the okay. And if Isa doesn't like the game . . . well, the job won't really like Isa. Rico will find a reason to get rid of her.

The game has been going on forever. It's a tradition as old as the restaurant. It's how my dad paid for his golf clubs in high school. It's how Cade Eisen made his first eight payments on his fancy BMW before he totally pulled an epic wuss-out and it got repossessed.

And it's how I, Xavi Diane Mitchell, am going to get the ever-loving hell out of this godforsaken town and move to New York City, where I will wear stiletto heels and fancy scarves and say things like "take the tube."

Wait, do people say "tube" on the East Coast, or is that, like, a British people thing?

Whatever. If it's not a thing, I'll make it one. I'm going to be a fashion designer, like Kate Spade or Betsey Johnson.

I stash my lipstick in my apron, grab a tray, and head out to the floor. I might as well start cleaning off table two if I'm going to have any chance at buying in.

People are so disgusting. I mean, what did they do here? Turn into Picasso, using the ketchup and hollandaise sauce? And oh my *damn*, someone has actually stuck their black cloth napkin to the window with leftover truffle butter. People are monsters. They're, like, not even people.

Yep, I bus, which is a shitty job, but Rico won't make me a waitress until I'm seventeen. Only four tiny months away. I tried to convince him to let me move up early, but he's a total stickler. I even tried to kiss him once, out back behind the Dumpsters, but he just misunderstood and hugged me. Seriously. Hugged. Like I was his little sister. So embarrassing. And so not helpful in moving me to waitress.

But it's not all bad. I mean, the waitstaff likes me and throws me a pretty big portion of their tips—so I can buy in for the game sometimes.

I finish busing the table, load all of the leftover dishes onto a tray, and lift it above my shoulder. I wave a hello index finger to Jake and Finn as they arrive for their shifts through the front door, work uniforms slung over their arms. Servers are supposed to use side doors. Finn must be wiped to be lazy enough not to park in back—I heard he worked pretty late last night with Isa, the new girl. Jake, well, he doesn't give a shit, even though he looks out of place among the long, wispy curtains and expensive art. But, I mean, the best parking is out front.

Jake is this skinny, rock-star-wannabe type, and I would

think he were cute if he actually showered. Finn is actually really attractive—probably because he spends every minute he's not waiting tables at football practice or the gym or whatever, getting all sweaty and pumping iron, probably wearing a tight shirt. Or maybe no shirt at all. He's kind of strange, and I think that's what I like about him. He's real because he doesn't get any other way to be.

"What's up, girl? How's my favorite blonde?" Jake asks. He wraps his orangutan arms around me, almost making me drop my tray. I hold my breath against his stink. Ugh. Fortunately, he's a dishwasher, so he's not exactly up-close-and-personal with the diners. And usually he smells a little more like actual soap by the time he ditches at the end of the night.

"We have customers," I hiss. There is a couple who arrived late for lunch enjoying early afternoon cocktails in the corner. Total lushes. I bet they'll be smashed by three.

Jake pulls away and pretends to pout. "Come hang with me in the kitchen, pretty."

Ugh. I kind of don't want to. But I've wiped down the window and I don't have any reason to be on the floor, so I hoist my tray a little higher and follow him. I need to unload the dishes for him anyway.

I follow him back, setting the tray carefully on the empty countertop next to the dishwasher, and Jake ties a stained apron around his waist. He pulls his too-long hair into a pony-tail and begins filling the sink to soak a couple of the dishes before putting them in the dishwasher. After he adds soap, I flick him all playful-like with a couple of handfuls of bubbles, hoping to make him smell a little less like a dead animal, and his eyes light up. He scoops up a handful of bubbles and tosses them back at me, but—they're more wet than actually bubbly, and they slop across the front of my shirt.

"Oops," he says.

Uh-oh. Pigsty thinks I'm flirting.

I look down at the wet mark on the front of my crisp white button-down.

"Jake!" I squeal. "I have to go back out there!" I paw at the spot, which is practically translucent. I mean, you can see skin. If I were attending, like, one-tenth of a wet T-shirt contest, I'd totally be eligible to enter.

"Is there a problem in here?"

I whip around.

Peter.

My stupid, stubborn stepbrother, Peter, who everyone thinks is *so. Cool.*

(News flash: He's not.)

"No," I say.

"Are you sure he wasn't spraying you?" Peter asks.

Oh my damn. Is he serious right now? Is he really playing the overprotective stepbrother card again? I mean, he's hardly even my stepbrother. He's been, like, just a guy at school I barely knew until our parents decided to go all lovey-dovey on us and get hitched after two months of dating. Ew.

"What are you, the water police?" I snap.

Jake holds up his hands. "We were just messing around, man. I swear."

Peter just stares at him, with his ridiculous intense eyes, and Jake sort of melts into a puddle of shame, like he's been shot with X-ray beams. Ugh.

I push past Peter and out, to the empty smoking patio reserved for employees. I wish, more than anything, that my stupid stepbrother hadn't started working here last year. I mean, it was fine before our parents got married, but now— now everything's different.

"Xavi," he says, following me out. "You okay?"

I glare at him. "Leave me alone. You're not even my real brother. I'll put up with you until our parents end up starring on *Divorce Court* or something, but don't pull the bullshit family card, okay?"

He waits for a moment, but I don't address him, so he closes the door behind me all quiet while I seethe.

Peter ruins everything.

Peter
Friday

At one point or another, everyone falls in love. It's totally normal. It's perfectly healthy.

But it's usually not with your stepsister.

It sounds terrible when I say it like that. But it's not. I've known Xavi for years, and she's always been just okay about me, and I've always had this little thing for her. And then our parents got married. And now she thinks I'm basically the Luke to her Leia. Or whatever slightly less dorky reference you prefer. It's like she thinks her mom is trying to replace her with me, like I'm the son the family needed or something, and it's created all of this resentment.

Not so conducive for a relationship.

Fortunately, I have a plan.

Rico is helping me. He just doesn't know it. I mean, I'm not going to tell him. I don't think it's socially acceptable to tell people you sort of want to bang your stepsister.

"You in for Tips tonight, man?" Rico asks. Rico's the boss. He always dresses like James Bond and does his hair like— well, Bruce Willis, seeing as he doesn't have any to speak of. And he's only thirty. He's standing in the kitchen with me, watching me cook. He says it's health code shit, but I'm pretty sure he's just bored. He doesn't actually do much in his own restaurant, besides overseeing the Tips game.

"What about Isa? The New Girl Rule?"

Rico grins. "I like Isa. We'll take a chance on her. Hey, man, you want a drink?"

I nod. He doesn't actually know we swipe liquor all the time, but if he did find out, I'm not totally sure he'd *care*. He's a decent boss and everything, but he likes a good time too. Like everybody. He leaves the kitchen while I begin peeling the sweet potatoes for the dessert special this evening (sweet potato pie with a brown sugar crust). The peels land in the bottom of the sink. Jake hates when I do this, but Celia's dishwashing tonight. She won't care. I sort of wish Jake were here. I'd leave all of them in there for him until they are damp and falling apart and let him deal with it.

Asshole.

Rico returns a minute later and slides me the smallest pour ever of—something. I sniff it. Crown. Like, two tablespoons of Crown.

"Uh, thanks, man," I say. He sits on the counter, which breaks about eighty of his precious health codes, and we clink glasses.

"Cheers." He has this slick look on his face, and I have a feeling he's about to tell me why.

"To Tips," I add, and we both drink. I set the empty glass down and begin peeling the potatoes again without saying anything. I know Rico. He'll spill.

He just looks at me, though, over his glass, and he keeps swirling his Crown like it's a nicer drink than it is. Unless it's the special reserve. But I doubt it.

"You ever worried about serving to minors?" I ask. I'm seventeen, but I can usually pass for nineteen. Bouncers rarely hassle me when I use a fake ID, and when I tend the bar, no one even questions me. The cops don't give us trouble as long as we take a few dollars off their tab at the end of the night.

He shrugs. "I don't hire idiots. And I only serve to employees." He grins so widely I can see gold on one of his back teeth. Gross.

"To responsibility." I lift my glass in a mock toast.

He laughs and then taps a finger against his lips. "How are the pies?" he asks.

"I made an extra one for the fridge," I tell him. I baked it last night, because Rico always gets into the pies, and I hate it when he takes one I've just made and then I have to go back and start the recipe over—for one pie. "You know, I think we need the menu updated. Can you get Dubois back in here? This is about the tenth time I've made these."

I'll admit it. I'm kind of protective of the restaurant—especially the kitchen. If I hadn't already sworn to my dad I'd go to school for IT, I wouldn't mind eventually ending up a chef somewhere, and Chef Dubois is kind of the shit. The fact that he ended up at Waterside blows my mind when he could be in New York or LA or something. But I guess he likes the small town and the bay. At least, when he's actually here, he looks out the window in front a lot and mumbles about the salt air. He's a weird dude, but I respect him.

"I'll reach out," Rico says. He hops down from my counter and opens the giant silver refrigerator.

"Third shelf," I tell him. I peel the last of the potatoes and lean back against the sink. He pulls out the pie and peels the plastic wrap off the top.

"Can I?" he asks, pointing at it. I had drawn an *R* on the top with whipped cream. You'd think that would be enough of a hint. I sure didn't make it for Raj, the valet, who always lies about his take.

"Whatever, man. You're the boss." I grab a fork and hand it to him. "Take it home."

"Thanks. You sure you have enough for tonight?"

"Sure."

He digs in with his fork and groans.

"Oh dear lord, Pete. This is the shit. I'm going to fire Dubois and let you take over the menu."

I laugh, wiping my hands on my apron. "I'm not quite ready for that yet."

Rico shakes his head. "This pie says you're a freaking Paula Deen, man."

I roll all of the potatoes into a bowl for mashing. I'm a racist old lady? Awesome. I choose to take it as a compliment. "Thanks, I guess."

For a while he lets me mutilate the potatoes in silence, but he's being, like, 10 percent creepy, the way he keeps watching me. He reminds me of Jake being weird with Xavi, and it raises all the hair on my neck. I wonder what she's doing. Who she's with.

"What?" I finally snap, and then regret it. Maybe snapping isn't the best way to relate to a boss.

"I've decided," he says simply.

"Decided what?"

He leans forward. "You're out of the game tomorrow."

I try my damnedest not to grin. This guy is playing right into my hands. "Should I assume I make the dare?"

He nods. "We've got over a grand in the pot after the weekend."

"It's time to play, then."

"Hell yeah. It's time to play."

Isa
Friday

"Isa!" Rico shouts, poking his head into the dining area.
"Get in here!" He crooks a finger at me and disappears behind the silver double doors that separate the floor from the kitchen.

I smile apologetically at Gustavo, a short kid who I'm helping bus the most disgusting table I have ever seen. Spitballs? Really? I mean, this is supposed to be a fine dining establishment. Not Applebee's during happy hour. "You cool to finish up?"

"I'm cool." He tries to smile back, but instead he looks like he might actually throw up. Which is where I was a minute ago when I was trying to pick up a phlegm-covered bit of napkin with a butter knife. I am pretty sure that single moment was worth roughly a billion points in karmic energy.

I wash my hands quickly at the kitchen sink and then head into Rico's office, which is more of a glorified supply closet, really. I'm not totally sure why he needs an office since there's actually nothing in there except for a dingy desk covered in candy wrappers and a few manila folders. A trash can with crushed soda cans sits neglected in the corner.

The only kind of cool part of his office is the ladder against the back wall, which leads to the roof. I heard that sometimes the employees go drink up there after hours, but I've never been invited. Well, not yet. I'm still pretty new. I'll give everyone a little more time before I write them off as assholes.

"What's up?" I ask. I sit down in the wooden chair opposite Rico, who, for once, is looking sort of serious. He's usually grinning at me in this way I find a little alarming, like I'm not sure if he's being friendly or being, you know—*friendly*.

"Isa," he starts, very slowly. He takes a deep breath, steeples his fingers, and then unsteeples them. He actually seems a little . . . nervous.

"Yeah?"

"How are things going? On the floor?" He's breathing fast.

"Um. Fine, I guess." I watch him through narrowed eyes. It's like he's . . . up to something. Something weird.

"And the money?"

"The money isn't bad." Actually, the money is pretty great. We get pretty incredible tips just because the food is so high priced. But I'm not about to let him think I'm content. Because I'm not.

I need more.

"I'd like to offer you . . . a more lucrative opportunity." He leans forward slightly in his chair, and the leather squelches underneath him.

"Lucrative?" I say. "You mean, more money? You're giving me a raise?"

He finally grins at that. "Yes, more money. But no raise. I mean, you've been working here for about twenty-four hours."

I lean back in my chair and cross my arms over my chest. Really? It's been, like, a week now. I don't get it. What's he talking about? A creepy prostitution ring he runs as a hobby in his spare time? A spot on his wannabe vigilante gang?

"Then what?" I ask.

"I'm talking," he says delicately, "about a little game. Something of a wager. Something all of my employees do. It's called Tips."

"Tips?" It sounds familiar. In fact, I'm pretty sure I heard Xavi discussing it with Finn on the back patio a couple of days ago, but they got all quiet and weird when I came over and started talking about the weather, and then Xavi started puffing on an unlit cigarette.

"Tips is a game that's been running for about thirty years. Every two weeks, the staff contributes about 20 percent of their tips into a pot for a chance to take an unknown dare. A task or stunt, if you will, that isn't revealed until the night of the game. One staff member stays out of the game each week and crafts the dare. And the rest of you—well, those who want to take the challenge . . . come forward. Everyone writes their initials on cash and drops it into a hat. If your bill is drawn, you accept the dare. And if you complete the dare, you win the entire pot."

"So, everyone just contributes a huge chunk of their tips on the chance they get the dare?"

Rico nods. "It's a very big pot. Trust me . . . if you win once, it's worth it. Oh, and to encourage our newest employees to participate in our extra-special culture here at Waterside—any first-time players get first dibs on the dare. But it's a one-time thing. One chance to accept the dare automatically, without your name being drawn from the hat, but after that you take your chances like everyone else."

Hmmm. That's interesting.

"And if you don't complete the dare?" I ask.

"Money goes back into the pot, and you're ineligible for the next time, but you still have to pay your fees." He grins, a little evilly, and moves back and forth in his swivel chair, like a villain in a bad spy movie.

I make a face. "So this is like truth or dare."

He shakes his head. "We don't require truth around here, Isa."

"And what are the dares? Like, toilet paper someone's house? Plastic wrap on the toilet seat?"

Rico runs his hand over his head. "I think you'll find us a little more creative than that."

I rub my hands together. "How much money are we talking, Rico?"

Rico pushes away from his desk and kneels down by the air-conditioning vent in his wall. He loosens the screws by hand and pulls out a fat stack of bills. He tosses them across the desk, leaving the vent cover on the floor. "This Saturday's take."

I feel my mouth drop open. I shut it quickly. He walks around and sits back in his chair, looking satisfied.

"You like?" he asks.

Of course I do.

It's more than I'd make in tips all summer. It's more than I've ever won, even in my biggest, most embarrassing beauty pageants.

"I, of course, supplement slightly with a few of my profits." He waves his fingers over a couple of the larger bills. "I like to see the game continue."

I raise my eyebrows. It seems like pretty easy money. "Nice."

"So," Rico says. He leans forward, onto his elbows. A few

dollars are pushed off the desk, onto the ground. "Are you in?"

I pick up the dropped bills and fan them out. I think of my parents, out on the road all the time. I think of my room in the back of my great-aunt's double-wide. I think of clothes from Walmart and off-brand granola bars and always being a little hungry. I think of making it all worth it.

It's not a hard decision.

"I'm in."

Rico's smile stretches even wider, reaching its normal creepiness levels. Strangely, I feel a little more comfortable. "Tips is always on Saturday nights. Be here at three a.m. Enter through the back door—it'll be unlocked. The game always starts on the roof. Come through this office, climb up the ladder, and you'll find us waiting."

"Awesome." I smile back at Rico, and a rather uncomfortable shiver runs a cold thread from my back up to my hairline.

"You can go," he says, like he's dismissing me, and he starts scrapping all of that gorgeous money back into a neat pile.

I stand up, and the wooden chair squeaks over the floor.

"Wait," Rico says suddenly.

"Hmm?"

"You're going to want to leave that money."

I look down and realize I'm still holding the fanned-out bills. I wave them at my face a couple of times.

"I do declare," I say with a hint of southern accent, "it must have slipped my mind."

I leave the cash on his desk and Rico laughing at my back.

Finn
Saturday

"Isa's weird." I join **Xavi** on the back patio with a handful of artichoke hearts I swiped from the salad bar.

"What do you mean?" She unties her apron and tosses it across a planter.

I shrug. "I'm never sure if she's going to kill me or if she's about to bust into a striptease." I pop an artichoke heart into my mouth.

Xavi wrinkles her nose at me. "I'm guessing neither."

"Seriously, Xavi." I lean against the railing on the patio and look out over the water. A fish jumps, and the sound of the splash carries over to us. Xavi turns her back to the railing and puts an unlit cigarette between her lips. "Rico shouldn't be letting her into the game so quickly. We don't know what she's about. Something's off there."

"Something's off here," she says, pointing to my head and making a circular motion around my ear. But she's smiling as she says it. "Besides, I heard you basically asked her to do you and that's why she doesn't like you. Smooth, Finn. So Don Juan of you."

I grin. I'm not exactly sure who Don Juan is, but I get it.

"Complete misunderstanding. I'm innocent, I swear."

"Right." Her voice is thick with sarcasm.

"What's your thing?" I point at her cigarette. "Why don't you ever light them?"

She winks at me. "Oral fixation, Finn."

"Well, don't tell that to Jake. He might take it the wrong way." I'm not kidding, either. Dude has a serious thing for Xavi. I found a messed-up love poem in his car about how his love for her was like roses and moonstones or some shit. It drives Peter crazy. He's way overprotective for someone who has only been her stepbrother for a couple of months.

Xavi fake-puffs on her cigarette. "Maybe if Jake tried a cologne outside of eau de cat piss, he'd get a girl. In the meantime, please don't mention it, mmm-kay?" She offers me a half smile, and I go back to staring at the bay. The sunset is pretty amazing—casting oranges and yellows off the water, like it's on fire or something.

"Are you in for tonight?" Xavi asks.

I frown. "Tonight?"

"Um, Tips is happening? Are you going to miss it?"

I laugh. Right. "Come on, Xavi. You know I never miss Tips. That's crazy."

And I don't. Tips is awesome. It's not like I need the money—I have other means of income, and plenty of it. But the thrill . . . There's nothing like it. Once, last year, I won by getting these giant purple hickeys from everyone at Tips that night, and then the next day I had to skinny-dip at the PTA picnic that Waterside Café sponsored.

It. Was. Epic.

Of course, Tips is also how I landed my other . . . gig. Let's just say that if a football scholarship doesn't work out, I've got college covered. If I get in. Grades aren't really my thing.

"I haven't decided if I'm playing," Xavi says. She toys with her cigarette, rolling it between her thumb and index finger and then putting it back between her lips.

"Why not?"

"Isa's playing. And if Isa decides she wants the dare this time, then New Girl Rule—she gets the dare, no questions asked. I might come hang out and just enter next time. I want it to be worth it."

I get it. Xavi doesn't have a lot of money. Waitstaff only have to contribute 20 percent of their weekly take, but Xavi has to give about 80 percent if she wants to even get in the neighborhood of the buy-in. Busgirls aren't exactly the highest paid folks at Waterside.

"What if I cover you?" I ask. It's not like I can't afford it. And Xavi wants to play. I can see it in her eyes. She's desperate. And I like Xavi. She's a girl you could trust.

She turns to face me. "You'd do that?" she asks. "Seriously?"

"Of course."

She turns away. "I can't."

"But Xavi . . . I could spot you. Just pay me back when you win."

She stares out at the water. The sun is dropping faster now, and the glare off the bay is bright and sharp. "If I enter, it'll be with my money. Okay, Finn?"

"Sure."

"You're sweet to offer, though." She tucks her cigarette carefully behind her ear.

"You know," I say, "you really could light that thing. See what nicotine is like."

Xavi gives a short laugh. "Are you crazy? I don't want to get cancer."

The patio door opens, and Rico pokes his head out. "Finn, you done with your break? One of your regulars is here."

I sigh. I've hardly been out here, and I have a feeling my shift is going to run late. I want to be on my game tonight. "Which one?" I ask.

"Patrick Clayton. I can give him away if you don't want him, though." Rico looks back inside. "Warren's here, and he has a five-top and a two-top—that's it."

Patrick Clayton. The owner of Daylon Industries, makers of fine neon hunting vests everywhere. In other words, made of money. He has a giant house on the other side of the water with a fountain out front.

"I'll take him, Rico," Xavi says cheerfully, but Rico shakes his head and grimaces.

"You can bus later, Xavi," he says. "I don't want to disappoint Clayton."

Her mouth settles into a pout—the kind of pout that's definitely practiced.

"I'll do it," I say. Rico shuts the door and disappears inside, and Xavi turns her pout face on me.

"Why do you think he won't let me be a waitress?" Xavi asks.

"Because you're sixteen," I say. "You'll get there. I'm sure you'll be promoted as soon as you turn seventeen."

"Then summer's over," Xavi says. "And the game's off. I need the money, Finn."

I put a hand on Xavi's shoulder. "I'm sure you'll figure it

out." I check my cummerbund and smooth my shirt before heading inside and out onto the floor. It's good to make customers wait for a little while.

Can't have them thinking I'm too eager.

There's something about waiting tables that I enjoy. I pretend to hate it, like everyone does, but there's something about the scripted-ness of the whole thing, about always knowing what you're expected to do and say.

And about doing none of it. At least, not in the way that people expect.

I find Patrick Clayton seated at a small table in the corner. As usual, he is dining alone, and his menu lies over his place setting, untouched. His napkin is already spread over his lap and his silverware is laid out neatly.

"Good evening, Mr. Clayton. Would you like to hear our specials?"

He clears his throat and straightens his tie. His gray hair is messy and he looks sort of tired—worse off than the last time I saw him. His wallet lies casually on the table, a few bills poking out of the top.

"No, Finn. No specials tonight."

I nod. "Would you care to have a look at our menu?"

"I'll just take the usual." He gives me a tight smile.

The usual. Of course.

I nod. "Let me just put this in to the kitchen."

Xavi
Saturday

I pull out the fold of bills from the last five weeks and count them again.

Is it worth it?

Rico needs the cash today. But if I buy in and lose . . . well, then, I'll basically be relying on my mom for cash, which is like relying on the crazy lady who sleeps in the shopping cart off seventh for mental health advice—aka, not happening.

I put my feet up on the long footrest running under the bar and count the money out for the fortieth time. I could enter. I have enough.

Or I could wait.

I tap my fingers on the bar.

I need the money. I need it if I want to get out of this hellish tourist town and to the East Coast. I need it if I want to go to design school and not some boring-ass state college, like my mother wants. But if I win this summer, and next . . .

Then *maybe* . . .

"You in tonight?" Peter asks. He's moonlighting as a

bartender while Rico's out doing God knows what. It's late enough that the kitchen is closed, and Jake's in charge of cleaning up tonight. Peter scrubs the surface of the bar with a fresh white rag.

"For Tips, you mean?" I ask. "Maybe. Haven't decided."

"What's stopping you?" he asks. He pours a glass of root beer and slides it across the bar to me. I catch it before it can fall off the edge. Smooth, Peter. Really. Whenever he's behind the bar, he likes to fake like he's one of those bartenders that can juggle bottles and shit. Mostly he just makes a huge mess and wastes a lot of liquor. A couple of months ago he flipped an entire bottle of merlot onto this blonde wearing a white dress, and she basically had a giant, celebrity-level meltdown.

They still ended up in full-on make-out mode by the end of the night. Chances are she left wearing nothing but a tablecloth.

Peter can be kind of a slut, but it's apparently okay because he's a guy.

"Isa's stopping me," I tell him honestly. I take a sip of my drink. "New Girl Rule. What if she takes the dare on her first time? You know that a new girl trumps all other entries. They'll be no drawing. She'll automatically get to take the dare. Then I have no chance and all this"—I wave my hand at my money—"is gone."

Peter glances at my cash. Everyone knows that bussers totally get shafted in a bad way around here. "I could spot you."

"Uh. No. Thanks." Like I'm going to be indebted to my asshole stepbrother. I'd rather take my chances with Hitler.

He shrugs. "Just an offer. I know you're good for it."

30

Oh my damn, why are people offering me money? Do I look like a charity case? I glance at the cash spread across the table. Well, maybe I kind of do. I gather it up and put it very carefully back in my apron. "Obviously, I am."

Peter stops wiping down the bar and puts his hands on the counter in front of me. "I have an idea."

I'm torn. I kind of don't want to listen to him, but this money is my chance to get rid of him forever, or at least a ticket out of here until my mom goes all Hollywood again and gets tired of his stupid dad, like she has of the three husbands before him. It's only a matter of time.

And being indebted to Peter? Ugh. Gag reflex.

I sigh. "What's your idea?"

"It's my turn to make up the dare. So what if I came up with a dare that Isa would hate? To make sure she wouldn't take it?"

"Hmm." But how could Peter know enough about Isa to know what she absolutely can't stand? But then . . . for some insane reason, girls gravitate toward Peter. They can't get enough of him. It doesn't make sense. He's actually kind of dorky. But Isa's probably just another one of the bugs caught in his weird Peter web.

I grab a cherry out from behind the bar and pop it into my root beer glass. Peter half smiles.

"What?"

He shakes his head, and his stupid rock-star hair sort of swings around his face. "That's kind of charming."

I stare at him. "Huh?"

"The cherry-in-root-beer thing. It's cute." He looks at me. Like, really looks at me. "No one else does that."

Ugh. What is wrong with him? I stare back, and he turns a little pink and clears his throat.

"Anyways, uh. How often does a new girl actually go in on a dare? Never happens the first time. No new girl yet has taken advantage of the rule, so I'd say you have a decent chance tonight. And if I make my dare involve Finn—well, then, I can't see Isa wanting to have much to do with it."

Maybe Peter actually has a point. As much as I hate to admit it . . . maybe tonight's not a bad time to buy in. And if Peter is actually going to help me . . . well, he's *sort of* influential. For some unknown reason, he's like the Judge of Cool around here. And Isa does have a serious hate-on for Finn.

But if I lose, who knows when I'll have the cash to pay my way in again?

I reach into my apron to feel the thick fold of bills.

"Why are you helping me, Peter? What are you up to? I mean—what do you want from me?"

For a second Peter just has this absolutely wicked grin on his face. And then it's gone, and his face is . . . honest. Calm.

"Look. I know things have been weird since our parents decided to go all midlife crisis on us and morph into horny teenagers. And it's been even weirder to be in the same house all of a sudden. But we used to be friends, didn't we? We used to have fun here before they ruined everything. So maybe . . . maybe I'm doing this for us. For old times."

Is he serious right now? I narrow my eyes at him and give him my best girl up-down. "Really, Peter?"

"What?" He frowns.

"I thought you were all about this *Brady Bunch* crap. Yay, blending families! Yay, let's all hold hands and sing "Kum Ba Yah" and watch *The Price is Right*!"

He crooks an eyebrow at me. "*The Price is Right*? That's your show of choice?"

I smile. I don't want to, but it comes to my face, unbidden. "Whatever. I've always had a thing for Bob Barker. Drew Carey. You know. Whatever old guy gives away the Chevy Malibus." I wave my hand at him.

"Right. Well." He cracks open his own bottle of root beer and toasts me. "Screw being siblings, Xavi. It sucks."

"Cheers to that."

He clinks his bottle against my glass and we drink.

"You know," I say, "there are some times in my life that you aren't the worst person in the world."

He laughs at that, and rests his forehead on the bar for a moment. I knock on the faux granite, and his head lifts. His dark eyes meet mine.

"What the hell are you doing, weirdo?"

"That's the nicest thing you've said to me since our parents got hitched." He looks goofy, his hair all over the place and a silly smirk on his mouth.

"Yeah, well, I aim to please." I grin at Peter and take another drink.

He winks at me. "After tonight, I promise you will be pleased. I have a good feeling."

"Me too."

Rico comes in through the kitchen, throwing open the silver doors grandly. He sees me sitting at the bar and ignores me completely.

"Peter! Tips?" He lifts his arms in a grand motion. "Two hours and counting!"

"I make the dare tonight," Peter says, grinning. "So absolutely."

"Xavi?" Rico turns toward me, drumming his hands on the bar. "Not in tonight?"

"Actually," I say, pulling out the cash and setting it casually on the bar, "I'm buying in."

Rico counts the money expertly. "Seems to be in order. See you on the second floor in a bit, then?"

"Yeah."

Rico pockets the cash. "Should be a good pot tonight, Xavi."

Peter gives me a cheesy thumbs-up behind Rico's back, and I bite back a smile.

Maybe my stepbrother isn't quite so bad.

Peter
Sunday
3:00 a.m.

I watch Xavi in the firelight.

She's beautiful. She's laughing, her hand on Finn's arm. Jake stands behind her with a half-empty beer. He didn't have the cash to buy in. He never does—he's just along for the ride. Plus, he pitches in a few dollars for the pot here and there, so no one tells him to leave.

Tips is nothing if not entertaining.

Xavi tosses her hair, and it tangles. The wind is stronger up here on the roof. She meets my eyes for a second and notices me watching.

And then she smiles. And her eyes move away.

She smiled. At me.

Tonight—tonight is going to be perfect.

I sit in a lawn chair—one of many we've set up on the roof, encircling a big-ass fire pit. God knows how many fire codes we're breaking up here. Rico has a five-gallon bucket of water sitting nearby in case anything gets out of control. Well, the fire. People up here are always out of control.

"Hey."

I look up to find Isa standing above me, a small purse

slung over her shoulder. She sucks her cheeks in and then lets her breath out slowly.

"Hey, Isa. Have a seat." I motion at a rather threadbare lawn chair, and she sits down in it very carefully. "It's stronger than it looks," I add, and she gives me a grateful smile.

"So this is Tips, huh?" she asks, setting her purse down by her ankles. "This is . . . different."

"What, you mean that it looks like a bunch of teenagers getting drunk on a rooftop?" I feign shock. "How dare you. This is a proper event. We'll have croquet on the lawn after."

"You're weird," she says, laughing.

"Also, want a beer?" I reach over and grab her a drink out of the cooler.

Isa shakes her head. "No, thank you. I want my head on straight tonight."

"Ah. Well. Word of advice?" I reach into the cooler again and come out with a bottled water with the label half falling off. She takes it gratefully.

"I need all the advice I can get."

I lower my voice and lean into her ear. "Don't go in your first time."

Her eyebrows draw together. "What? Why?"

"Tips can be—ah—tricky, you know? Best to observe from afar. To see how it's done, and then try it out. It's just how people do it. No one actually goes in their first time—it's too risky. If you change your mind, Rico's collecting final entries now. But . . . watch. Learn."

Isa nods. "Thanks, Peter," she says, earnestly. "I feel like you're the game guru here."

"No prob. You sure you don't want a beer?"

She shakes her water bottle at me. "I think this is about all I can handle right now."

"Sure." I take a sip of my own beer and grimace. It's gotten warm despite the relative coolness of the night—probably from being too close to the fire pit. I down it quickly and pick at the curling end of the label.

"You know what that means, right?" Isa asks.

"What *what* means?" I'm not really paying attention. I'm watching Xavi again. She used to joke with me the way she's joking with Warren, one of the college-age waiters who picks up bar shifts sometimes. She used to smile at me all the time—not just across a campfire when I'm about to do a gigantic favor for her. She made me believe I had a chance.

She made me believe that she could love me.

Isa uncurls a finger from her water bottle to point at my hands. "Playing with your beer label. It means you're sexually frustrated."

"Oh?" I say. "Tell me more." I flirt with her on autopilot, but my eyes are still on Xavi. She looks my way again, but this time she doesn't smile. In fact, she stands up and goes to talk to Rico.

"You and Xavi aren't the best of friends, huh?" Isa asks.

I shake my head. "We're fine."

Isa cocks her head sideways at me, and for a moment I feel totally laid bare, like she's seeing everything I've ever felt about Xavi. But she just blinks and goes, "Huh."

"What about you?" I ask. "How do you like it here?"

She surveys the little crowd. "It's . . . interesting, I guess. People seem nice. Beats my other job."

"What other job?"

Isa hesitates and takes a long sip of her water. "Just something stupid," she says. She shifts so her shoulders are slumped sort of inward, like she's protecting the core of herself. I decide not to press her. For some reason Isa doesn't strike me as someone particularly forgiving. Her face looks strange in the firelight: angry and pensive all at once. Not like the Isa who mischievously stole a lighter from my back pocket.

Rico stands suddenly, like he always does. He holds a beer in one hand and a glass of scotch in the other. He's changed from his trademark suit into cheesy board shorts and a gray T-shirt, sweat showing through at the chest and armpits, like he's been running before he came here. I imagine what he looks like at home—lying on the couch, maybe eating Cheetos while crumbs collect on his chest.

The circle quiets. Everyone stops talking, laughing, even moving. The only sounds are the crackle of the fire and a light breeze, rustling the trees near the shoreline. In the distance the grumbling sound of an engine starts, and then grows farther away until it's nothing. Isa tenses on the other side of me.

"Let's begin," Rico says. His voice has a grim edge to it—there is none of his normal bravado or self-importance. "Players tonight, please stand."

On the other side of the campfire, Xavi stands. Finn stands too. He'd never miss a game of Tips. Ever. Once he came with pneumonia. Warren stands, and a couple of other waitstaff—Jeremiah and Aida, who always request the late shift—stand too. Aida is a little wobbly from too much booze, and Jeremiah wraps his arm around her shoulders to steady her. Last, Celia, the dishwasher, rises. Everyone takes a step toward the fire pit. Those who aren't playing tonight step back.

"Peter?"

I stand too. But . . . Isa stands with me. She tilts her chin up as she does it, flashing me a triumphant look.

She's playing. A single bill dangles from her hand. She must think she might need to put more money in the pot to play.

Which means she's going to take the dare. Or, at least, she's considering.

But wait until she hears my dare. She'll be out in a second. I glance over at Finn, who is standing solemnly beside Xavi. I'd be more worried about him so near my stepsister if I didn't know for a fact he has never touched a single girl in our high school. Not to mention I don't think he'd ever mess around with my Xavi. We're friends, after all.

Rico clears his throat. "Tonight, Peter will state his dare. All interested parties will place their money in a hat for consideration." He pulls a rumpled baseball cap from his back pocket and hands it to me. I hit it against my hand a couple of times, trying to get it into some sort of shape that will actually hold cash.

"So what's the dare?" Rico asks.

I smile.

I've got this.

"You have to kiss, chosen by jury, the absolute worst person for you on this roof. Right now. In front of everyone. And I don't mean short pecks on the lips. I mean make out. For one full minute."

I pull a stopwatch out of my pocket.

Xavi wants the money. She won't back down. There's absolutely no way Isa will kiss Finn, and she knows the group will gladly push him forward. I'm not sure about Warren—he might stay in, because I'm pretty sure he'd make out with a doorjamb. And Finn will do anything. Everything. Aida and Jeremiah are likely out too, since they're both ridiculously jealous and Celia always chickens out. Which gives Xavi a decent chance . . . and she knows it. She's beaming at me from across the campfire. Sometimes the simplest dares take out the most players, and this super-easy kissing dare is going to be rough for a lot of people right now.

And of course—Xavi doesn't know this yet . . . at least, I don't think she does—but that means she'll have to kiss me.

I'm very obviously the worst person for her to kiss, being her stepbrother.

Everyone will choose me for her.

And I'm a very good kisser, when I want to be. Good enough to convince Xavi there's something there. Something between us. Something that maybe she's forgotten about since our parents got hitched.

Enough to make her think.

Hell, I'll volunteer.

Fuck what everyone thinks.

"May I remind you," Rico says, "that anyone caught documenting or photographing a dare in any way will never be allowed in the game again and will immediately be fired from employment at Waterside."

He pauses to walk around the circle of those still standing.

"Now anyone who wishes to drop this dare will sit."

Aida sits immediately and then tugs urgently on Jeremiah's hand until he sits too, a bit reluctantly.

Jealous couple, check and check.

Celia sits too, slowly. I feel a little bad for her. It must have taken her a long time to save up a buy-in. And to go out on a kiss? That's rough.

Anyway, shy dishwasher? Check.

Warren sits rather suddenly. Huh. Weird. Maybe there's someone else in his life that wouldn't appreciate him slipping tongue to another girl.

Frat boy player? Check.

That leaves Xavi, Finn—and Isa.

Isa takes a small step back and then swallows hard.

She looks around at the group.

If she takes this, then there will be no drawing. Isa will get the dare, no questions asked.

It's the power of the New Girl Rule.

"I'm in," she says.

Isa

Sunday
3:24 a.m.

I just took the dare. The first dare.

My hands shake at my sides. I clench them into fists.

And I think of the money.

The money that will be mine. Every last penny. Not going into a scholarship fund, not going to my parents.

Mine.

Peter looks shocked. His mouth is slightly open, and his face is pale. He didn't expect me to accept. Or he didn't want me to.

And Xavi—Xavi is still standing. And, for some reason, she's watching Peter, tears running down her cheeks. Angry tears. She wanted this.

And Finn—well, Finn sticks his hands in his pockets and grins at me.

"Alright, Isa," Rico says. "Peter will time, providing he isn't chosen to participate. Chicken out, pull away, or in any way render the dare incomplete, and the money stays in the pot for next time. Also, a wuss-out makes you ineligible to compete next time."

"I opt out!" Jeremiah says, raising his hand. "On the

grounds that Aida will literally slice my throat."

Aida nods very seriously behind him. "I will, too."

I swallow hard. Good. One down. "I'm not kissing Rico," I announce. No way am I going to do that. I'd rather gargle toilet cleaner.

"Rico's not allowed in the game anyway," Peter mutters.

That leaves Warren, Finn, and Peter. Fortunately, Jake, the smelly dishwasher, didn't buy in. I wouldn't mind kissing Warren or Peter. Warren's sort of cute in a frat-boy way, and Peter—well, Peter's adorable. And then, of course, there's—

"It's Finn," Peter says. His words are almost cruel, the way they spill over his lips. "She hates Finn."

"It's definitely Finn," Xavi agrees. She stares hate at Peter, and then her eyes shift to me. She crosses her arms over her chest. She is not happy with me.

She thought she was going to get this.

One by one, everyone on the roof agrees that I should kiss dumb, blond, sexist Finn. They say it with leering grins and reluctant agreement and complete, unadulterated glee.

Finn steps forward, and I walk over to him. My body shakes. God, this is so wrong. Why am I doing this? Am I really whoring myself out for money in front of a group of people? Is it worth this?

Finn grabs my hands and he leans in. For a moment, I think he's going to kiss me already, and I flinch. But he passes my lips and whispers to me.

"You don't have to do this, Isa," he says softly in my ear, so that no one else can hear. "You can back out. I won't be hurt."

For a moment, I want to listen. I want to push him away and run. I want to grab my purse and climb down the ladder to the restaurant. I want to leave and never come back.

But where will that leave me? Back at the trailer? Taking intermittent phone calls from my parents? Buying my clothes on clearance and faking that I have all the things everyone else does?

Finn draws away slightly, and I meet his eyes. I put my hands on either side of his face.

"Yes, I do. I have to do this."

He gives a little nod.

Peter clicks his stopwatch once, and I drop my hands to Finn's neck and pull him to my lips. He's surprisingly not forceful. He's almost—sweet. He kisses me very softly for a few seconds, tucking my hair back behind my ears, and then presses his hands into the small of my back. He bends me backward, deepening the kiss, and his tongue touches mine for a brief moment. Everyone whoops and catcalls in the background. I move my face against his, like I'm really into it.

He's not a terrible kisser, actually. He's pretty good. Not at all slobbery. I might actually enjoy it if I wasn't on display for the entire world.

Oh my gosh. I am enjoying lip locking with *Finn*.

Somewhere, deep beneath the earth's crust, Hell just got a skating rink.

"Time," Peter calls, and I hear the click of his stopwatch. I let go of Finn, breathing hard. My heart beats wildly. Finn grins at me.

"Judges?" Peter asks, but already everyone is clapping. Warren catcalls.

I wipe Finn off my mouth and do a little curtsy. Adrenaline courses through my blood. It wasn't so bad.

Rico claps a hand on my shoulder. "Nice going, new girl," he says. He hands me a fat manila envelope. "Enjoy."

I open the envelope and stare at the cash inside. The fold of bills is far thicker than it was yesterday. More people must have bought in. Or Rico supplemented more.

It won't fit into my tiny purse. I tuck it under my arm.

This isn't pageant money. My great-aunt didn't watch me win this, suffocating under pounds of makeup and endless yards of tulle.

I won this. Me.

"Don't stress," Warren says, nodding at the envelope. "No one would dare steal it. Rules." He grins at me. His blond-tipped hair is bright in the firelight.

"You think people wouldn't break that rule?"

"And ruin their chances forever if they got caught?" Warren laughs. "Trust me. People who play Tips can be a bit . . . maniacal. Tonight was tame, Isa. You got off easy. You wouldn't want to see how we'd tear apart someone who didn't honor the rules."

"So I'm fine," I say.

Warren pats me on the back. "You're good, Isa. Trust me."

Somehow, Warren's assurances start a nervous tickle in my stomach. Maniacal? All I had to do was kiss some asshole. And I've made bank.

There's nothing I won't do.

Finn
Tuesday

"I don't get it," Aida says, frustrated. **"What's your** secret, Finn? You have an uncle who's crazy rich or something?" She slams her tips onto the table. "Ugh. I'm never going to make my car payment this month. I'm fifty short."

We're at the back table of the restaurant during a lull, tallying our gratuities. She, like a few others, is in serious financial hardship because of her wuss-out during Tips. We're supposed to take extra out to tip the bussers. Not everyone always does, and I seriously doubt Aida will, so I usually try to slip them a little extra. Especially Gustavo. Xavi gets decent tips because she's gorgeous. She could probably be a model if she were seven inches taller.

"Did you really need a sports car?" I ask Aida. But she does what everyone does—assume they're going to win big at Tips and overspend. But Aida's too conservative for the game. She never has the guts to actually follow through.

And now she might lose her car.

She puts her head in her hands, and I slip an extra fifty into her pile while her eyes are covered. "Recount it," I advise. "Look in your couch cushions at home. Maybe you'll find something."

She makes a frustrated noise. "Couch cushions? Really? And I can't ask Jeremiah for more, Finn. Seriously. I get that not all your cash is from Waterside, but how do you get such amazing tips? Mine don't compare."

Sometimes it's all about money around here. And with Aida, it's all about Jeremiah or money. I almost feel bad for her. I'd bet my own wheels that Jeremiah gets rid of her before he heads to college in the fall. And she's not the best waitress I've ever seen. I'll be surprised if she lasts the summer.

"You really want to know?"

"Yes. I really *need* to know." She rests her chin in her hand and looks at me. "Tell me all of your secrets." She smiles that kind of smile that girls use when they fully expect to get everything they've just asked for.

There is no way she is getting my secrets.

Any of them.

I have an agreement.

Also, I'm not really into juvie.

"Well," I say, putting my elbows on the table, "you're kind of impatient with your customers. You have to treat them like they deserve all the time in the world. Like you'd treat your grandma."

"I do!" she says.

I shake my head. She definitely doesn't. Last week she told a table they needed to leave because she didn't like stupid people very much. She's just lucky Rico didn't overhear. And if that's how she treats her grandma, she has bigger problems.

"Well, after July, football starts back up. I'll have to cut my shifts to make practice, and you'll get more tables."

"Are you kidding me?" Aida says. She gathers up her tips and slips them back into her pocket. "Even on your off days, I get more people. And some diners come in and request you—and if you're not here to serve them, they *leave*. Like, they just book it. They don't even eat."

"Well," I say, "I'm good." I shrug, feeling sort of uncomfortable. I don't meet her eyes. "People like me."

She tosses her short blond hair back behind her shoulders. "People *like* Gandhi. But he wouldn't make as much waiting tables as you do."

I don't know who that is. I fidget with a napkin ring. "What can I say? When you're good, you know . . . you're good." I pretend to be cocky. It's easy when you're a football player. People expect you to be full of yourself.

And I don't know what else to tell her.

Aida gets really close to me and grabs my chin in her hand, forcing me to turn to face her. Her too-long nails dig into my skin. Rico will make her cut those before they get any longer.

"You're hiding something," she says. "Jeremiah thinks so too. You have a secret. Are you stealing? You're a thief, aren't you? I knew it!"

I push her hands away and stand up. "No! What kind of person do you think I am?"

She smiles. "Too close to home, Finn?" she asks, super sweet.

I shake my head, disgusted. And to think I just slipped her a fifty. "Not close at all, Aida. If you want more money, *try not being a jerk*. But don't come to me."

Isa appears over my shoulder. "The mayor's here, Finn. She's requesting you." Isa has actually been sort of polite since the whole kissing incident. And when I say sort of polite, I mean not over-the-top cruel. A few days ago, she might have conveniently forgotten to tell me the mayor had arrived, and she definitely wouldn't have said hi when I started my shift. With Isa and me, things are sort of looking up.

Not so much with Aida.

"Jamie's here?" I smile. I like Mayor Fields. She won't let anyone else wait on her. I turn back to Aida. "You want to know how to get bigger tips? You *care*, Aida. That's all. Something you're not great at right now."

I straighten my bow tie and my cummerbund and go to attend to the mayor, praying that Aida won't see through my lie.

If anyone cares to look close enough, I could lose everything.

Xavi
Thursday

"Damn it!"

A tiny drop of blood appears at the tip of my index finger. I stick it in my mouth. I can't keep my mind on this stupid dress. It's the fourth time I've poked myself. It's hard sewing with a thimble—or a bandage, for that matter—and I really, really don't want to mess this up. It's going to be beautiful. Short with a full baby-doll-type skirt and off-the-shoulder sleeves. Very electric. Completely amazeballs.

Or it would be if I could just sew right, without stabbing myself a billion times. I take my finger out of my mouth. I'm probably not going to bleed out and die, sprawled out on the floor from a microscopic stab wound, so I can do this. I can. I am going to finish it, and wear it, and bring it to New York City where it will be part of my new line, and then a billion girls will be wearing it next season.

I take a moment to look around my room. It used to look like an actual teenage girl lived here, but in the past year I've wallpapered every available inch with what I call inspirational clothes. My friend Julianna, who moved away last year, once told me to make a collage of all my dreams. So I started one, and then it basically became a monster and took over my entire room like some sort of aggressive flowering plant. It's weird, but my dad had always been the one to encourage me in fashion. I feel like this is my way of remembering him.

That and the photos in the corner. Mom thinks it's unhealthy. She calls it a shrine. But they're all photos of my dad. My family, when it was whole and my dad was alive.

I finish a few stitches and reach for the bottom layer of fabric that will bloom out of the skirt of the dress like petals. It's going to be gorgeous. I picked it up earlier today with the nearly nonexistent extra cash I had left over from going all-in for Tips. It was even on clearance, and there was just enough left to make this piece ridiculously amazing.

I spread the delicate fabric out over the table . . . and see a huge snag, running up and down the length of the material.

"Are you kidding me?" I groan. I hadn't noticed it in the store. I'd been so excited, I just bought it. I ball up the fabric and throw it against the wall. Why had I listened to Peter and entered Tips? I hate him. And now, I definitely can't swing buying more fabric. In all fairness though, I can't completely blame my a-hole stepbrother. It was my own fault too. I was stupid. Maximum levels of stupid. I could have put my big-girl panties on and waited two more weeks when I'd actually have enough money with enough left over to live if I lost.

I hate Rico, too. If he could just promote me to waitress already, I wouldn't be living like Little Orphan Annie, except, you know, with a house and a life and stuff. I'd have enough to be in the game every time, enough to buy fabric, and if I won—well, I'd be headed to design school. Exactly where my mother and new stepfather don't want me to go.

And I *would* win.

I'd do anything.

I pick up the material and spread it out across the table, then scream in frustration.

Above me, my stepfather pounds on the floor. "Quiet!" he roars. He's probably trying to watch his stupid NASCAR races. He's so different from Peter. My stepdad looks like he accidentally stepped straight out of a trailer park into a successful law firm. Whereas—Peter is Peter. He's cool. Or he would be, if he didn't suck so much.

I glance at my computer screen, and there's an IM blinking. Rico. Weird. I didn't even know I had Rico added to my IM list. I click on the blinking icon.

Sorry you lost last week, sweetie. ☹ Was rooting for you.

He's sorry? Really? And what's with the sweetie? Creeper alert much? Still, he's my boss, so I type back, Yeah, me too. That's honest.

I open a new browser window to check for more fabrics online, but my IM blinks again. Rico's back.

You seem a little more down than usual lately.

I'm a little lower on cash than usual lately. Maybe I shouldn't be so blunt with my boss, but I don't care. Nothing's going right anyway.

Oh?

What is that supposed to mean? Yes, I type.

Maybe I can help you with that.

Oh my damn. Does that mean he's going to promote me to waitress? After all the hell that being a busgirl has been, am I finally going to make real money? Will he hire another busgirl so I don't have to clean up dishes anymore?

My heart beats a little faster.

Really? I type.

Really.

Will you make me a waitress?

I press enter before I can chicken out.

He doesn't answer. At least, not right away. I go back to checking out fabrics, and another IM pops up on the screen.

Peter. Peter who lives upstairs from me. Why is my stepbrother IMing me when he could walk down a flight of stairs?

You okay? Heard you scream.

I shake my head. Really, Peter? Very brave of you to come downstairs and check. Because I will definitely answer an IM if I'm being murdered. I'll just ask very nicely for the gun/ax/weapon of choice to be put aside for two seconds while I check my screen. Killers definitely have their priorities straight, and IMing is one of them.

Fine, I type. Just frustrated.

What's wrong? He responds immediately. Too fast. Like he actually cares. I start to type an answer, but Rico's IM window lights up, so I close out of Peter's. He can wait.

Catch me early, before one of your shifts. We can talk.

And then, Peter's window lights up: Can I help?

To Rico: Sure

And back to Peter: No. Thanks.

Peter
Thursday

I knock on Xavi's door, my heart beating hard.

I'm being stupid. This is my house too. Not just Xavi's. It's not weird for me to visit my stepsister in her bedroom. Right?

Maybe it is when you want to see her naked.

"Come in, I guess," she says. I open the door slightly, and Nila, Xavi's gigantic, fluffy Persian, runs into the room and jumps into Xavi's lap, purring like a chainsaw missing half its teeth.

Xavi frowns at me.

"Hey," I say.

"Hey."

I stand awkwardly by the half-open door.

"Are you coming in, or what?" she asks.

I guess that means she's okay with me being in her room. She was jealous of my room, at first. I get why. Xavi has the same tiny room she's always had, and her mother transformed the gigantic bonus room into a bedroom for me—which means my room is double the size of hers. Plus, it's right over the garage, which is prime sneak-out real estate, and it's so far away from our parents' bedroom I could practically have a rager and they wouldn't know.

I wedge myself through the door and close it behind me. Wait. Should I have left it open? Or cracked? Does being closed make it inappropriate? We aren't related or anything, not really. I sit down on the very corner of her bed, and wonder, for a second, what it would be like to share it with her. To feel her curled into me while we sleep.

Xavi stares at me. She pets Nila mechanically, and the cat stares too.

"Are you okay?" I ask.

She gives me the girl look. You know the kind. The one that plainly says, without any question, *Are you insane?* I immediately want to vanish.

What is it about Xavi that makes me feel like this? No other girl—none—could make me nervous. Or have much of an effect at all.

"I mean, I heard you scream," I add.

"I'm fine," she says, cocking her head at me. "I found the most perfect fabric ever and it has an epic snag I didn't see in the store. It was on clearance, so I can't return it. So it's just basically the most useless thing to ever not use."

I'm not entirely sure she's speaking English. "Okay," I say, very slowly. "Can I help?"

"Unless you're a very fast-moving silkworm," she says, "no. No way." She tosses the fabric in the general direction of the trash can, but completely misses. Nila leaps off her lap and pounces on the fabric. "Nila, no!" she squeals, like she suddenly regrets her decision. "I was going to use that for accent pieces!" She dives toward the trash can, her hands outstretched, and Nila arches her back.

I kneel down beside Xavi and pick Nila up. "Here." I put my hands under Nila's legs, so her paws are outstretched, and Xavi begins carefully picking the fabric out of her cat's claws without screwing it up any worse. Nila swipes at her fingers while she works. I tighten my grip on the cat.

Nila growls, and while I can't be completely sure, I think it's Feline for *I'm going to kill you in your sleep*.

"Can't you just buy more?" I ask. The fabric looks like shit. There are tiny, visible holes where Nila got into it.

"Not really," she says. "It was the last piece. And I'm not exactly high-rolling at the moment. So yeah. No." There's more than just disappointment in her voice. There's sadness. And something else.

"It's just fabric," I say. "I mean, you can cut up one of my shirts, if you want."

She arches an eyebrow at me. "So you're just saying you have silk shirts on hand I can cut to pieces?"

I grin. "Actually, I do."

I run upstairs, rummage around in the Tupperware containers I shoved beneath my bed, and return a minute later, carrying two silk shirts—one a shiny green and the other hopefully matching the snagged silk.

"Are you kidding me right now?" she says as I dump them on her desk. "You own *silk shirts*?" She picks one up by the sleeve and holds it away from her body, like it might attack her.

I don't meet her eyes. Maybe this wasn't a great idea. "Can we pretend I wore them as Halloween costumes? We can say it was a *Saturday Night Fever* thing."

It wasn't. It was a really horrible decision from an even

worse band I was in four years ago. A band where we decided silk shirts would like the anticool or something.

And they were.

I will admit to neither the band or the undeniable fact I chose the shirts from a Goodwill store off Fourth Ave. *Chose* being the key word. *Painstakingly selected* is probably closer to the truth.

"What's *Saturday Night Fever*?" she asks, cocking her head at me in that cute way that she does.

I scratch behind my ear. "Uh, never mind that."

She picks up the second shirt. "This is *perfect*."

I can feel my ears turning red. "You can—uh—you can have it, Xavi. If you want it. Maybe it's not right. Both of them, I mean. You can have."

Now I'm not speaking English.

Xavi's lips part and she giggles at me. She bends forward, her hair falling into her face, and really *laughs*, like I've never seen her let go. I love it, even if it's at my expense.

She looks beautiful.

"Should I—uh—go?"

She shakes her head and sits down next to me on the bed. She's so close. Close enough to touch. Closer than I've ever seen her. There's a tiny scar on her chin. I wonder how she got it.

"No. Thank you, Peter. Seriously."

I want to kiss her. I study her lips.

"Can I tell you something?" she asks.

Holy shit. "Yeah." I lean in—just a little.

"I—I'm sorry for being such a bitch about losing Tips. You tried to help me. You wouldn't have known that Isa would be so gung ho about sticking her tongue down Finn's throat." She looks down at her hands.

"I'm sorry it didn't go better for you," I say. I nudge her leg. "But maybe you can enter next time."

She probably can't, though. She won't make enough cash and she won't take any money from me.

"Maybe I will," she says. "Rico wants to talk to me sometime this week about a money opportunity. He asked me to come in early and everything. I think he means promoting me to waitress."

I get a strange, jealous pit in my stomach. "He asked you to come in early?"

"Yeah. I mentioned I was a little low on funds and he said he could help me out. So it has to be a promotion, right? What else could it be?"

"I—I don't know," I say. But I don't like it. I've never seen it, but I've heard . . . rumors about Rico hooking up with his waitstaff. For "favors." The dude does give me the creeps sometimes.

"What?" Xavi demands.

"Just—be careful with him, okay? Rico's a little . . . creepy."

"*You* chill with him all the time."

"Yeah, but Rico's not trying to sleep with me. I hope. I've heard Rico can ask pretty girls to do some pretty shady shit when they need something from him."

Xavi's mouth drops open. "You seriously think Rico will actually ask me for some sort of *sexual favor* in exchange for a promotion? Damn, Peter. You are such a perv. Do you seriously think I couldn't make it on my own merits?" Her voice is cold, and a little hurt. She pulls a pillow off her bed and clutches it tight to her chest. A barrier between us.

"No, but I think Rico's stupid enough to try." I don't know why I'm telling her this. But I want to protect her.

Not hurt her.

She looks at me coldly and scoots away. "I think you should go."

"Xavi—that's not what I mean. I think you'd be a great waitress."

She glares at me. "I don't care. I remember why I don't hang with you. Leave. Come back in a few days and I'll tell you all about doing Rico in exchange for my waitressing job."

"I'm sorry." I don't know what else to say.

She looks at me, her pretty eyes like ice. "I don't care."

Isa
Friday

"Did you know," Peter tells me very seriously, **"that** there ain't no party like a Waterside party because a Waterside party don't stop?"

Xavi rolls her eyes and I giggle. "Um, no. I didn't actually know that. Thank you, though, Peter."

We just finished the late shift at Waterside, and Peter has convinced us to walk over to Finn's dock party. Apparently, Finn's grandpa has this epic houseboat and a huge dock where everyone goes to smoke joints and do shots. Finn always invites all of the Watersiders there to party, and usually before the end of the night it turns into a rager. I heard that last time, some girl from out of town almost drowned and Warren had to give her mouth-to-mouth on the beach. Not that someone almost dying counts as entertainment, but no one can say that Finn's parties are boring.

And I have to say—I might not have considered partying with him before the kiss.

"You have liquor, Finn?" I ask as we approach the already buzzing dock. He glances at Peter, who pulls out a half-empty bottle of Jack.

"Swiped it from the bar," Peter says with a wink. "Rico'll never notice."

"Gimme." Xavi holds her hands out, and Peter passes her the bottle. She takes a quick swig and grimaces. "Ugh. I always forget how much I absolutely hate whiskey."

"I'm fine with it," Finn announces. He snags the bottle from her and takes a longer draw, and then he passes it to me. I wipe off the lip of the bottle on the bottom of my shirt. I know Finn's had his tongue in my mouth, but I still have standards. I take a quick shot.

"Good girl," Peter says, looking at me approvingly. For some reason, I blush. He takes the whiskey back and takes a good slug himself, and then raises the bottle to the crowd of people on the dock.

I pick out a couple of people from the restaurant—Warren, Josh—the cook who works when Peter doesn't, Celia, and Jeremiah. Jeremiah without Aida clinging to his side like a cocklebur. Weird. I'm surprised she lets him pee without her.

"Hey!" Jeremiah says, lifting his arms. "What's up? Finn, gonna unlock the boat?" He points to a rather grand looking houseboat. A couple sits on the prow, sharing a joint.

Finn grins widely and holds up a set of keys.

"Where's Aida?" I ask Jeremiah.

He shakes his head. "Uh, she's sick. Girl problems." His eyes don't meet mine—they're on my neckline and creeping steadily lower. Ugh. Drunk and unsubtle. Excellent combination.

"Hey, Isa!" Warren crashes into me and wraps his arms around me like he hasn't seen me in a hundred years, when in actuality he was getting off work when I started. "You came!"

"Um, yeah," I agree.

He takes a sip of something from a blue Solo cup. "I'm DJing," he says. "Will you come help me choose the tunes?"

I nod and follow Warren and Finn onto the boat. Finn unlocks the door near the bow, and we step into the living room. It's unbelievably gaudy. The floor is a dull brown carpet, covered with thick, shaggy rugs. The couch is huge and purple leather, and everything is edged in bright gold.

Warren chuckles. "This place is sick, dude. Vintage madness."

What does that even *mean*? Vintage madness? Really? I try to keep the judgment off my face.

Finn points to a large stereo system in the back. "Fire it up," he tells Warren, who grins like a six-year-old with new finger paints.

"Dude!" Warren says excitedly, flicking on the equipment and attaching his iPod. I try to look over his shoulder at the music, but he ignores me. So much for helping him choose the tunes.

"Want a tour?" Finn asks me, and grins—a little devilishly.

I sidle up to him and touch his chest with the tips of my fingers. "What did you have in mind?" I ask breathily. "The bedroom?"

Half of his mouth perks up. "Sure."

I step back. "Yeah, Finn. No way." I toss my hair.

He stares at me for a couple of long seconds, and then laughs. "We'll save the tour for another time."

I wink. "Mark it on your calendar for never."

He laughs harder. Who would have thought—asshole jock Finn with good kissing skills *and* a sense of humor about himself?

It's like Rico with hair: wrong on so many levels.

Finn jerks his head toward the dock. "Let's go back out with the others." He snags a beer out of the fridge, pops it open, and hands it to me without asking.

"Thanks," I say. Nice of him.

"Watch for the pills tonight," he warns me as we climb out of the boat. He reaches back to steady me as I step onto the dock. "They're nasty. Chances are you'll do something really stupid, and the worst part is you'll remember it."

I toast him with my beer. "I think I'm good with this. Not really into the drug scene."

He shrugs and gives me a sort of friendly smile, and some woman—older, but stunning—accosts him. I stand on the edge of the dock, looking out over the water. The moon is out tonight, and it leaves a pale, trailing reflection on the water, all the way back to the horizon.

I feel, rather than hear, someone walk up beside me. The music is crazy loud now with Warren pumping old eighties tunes at full volume. I look over. Xavi.

"Hey, girl," she says. She sits down on the dock, and her feet dangle into the water. She's lost her shoes at some point. Xavi pats the spot next to her.

"Okay." I slip out of my flats, push up my slacks, and touch my toes to the surface of the water. It's deliciously cool.

"So, congrats," she says. She clinks her plastic cup against my beer, and we both drink. "Big win. Ready for the next one? It's a rematch."

"Of course," I say. "I'm buying in. You?"

She shakes her head. "You're talking to a class-A busgirl. Cleaning other people's shit doesn't exactly pay in gold. At least, not enough gold to get a girl entered in Tips every time it rolls around."

"Yeah," I say. "Sucks."

Xavi kicks the water, sending a spray of it through the air. "Whatever." She looks at me, considering. "Hey, what are you going to buy with all that cash? You won big, girl."

I did. I know I did. "I—uh—don't know. Like, makeup and stuff."

That's a lie. A bad one.

"Come on," Xavi says. "You've got some idea. Everyone does. That's why we enter."

I pull my feet out of the water. "Really, I don't. I think I just heard someone calling me. I'll be back."

That's another lie. I grab my flats off the side of the dock. Maybe this party wasn't such a good idea. I should stop drinking and just drive back home, where no one will bother me.

An arm suddenly links through mine.

Peter.

"Ever considered losing the cummerbund before partying?" he asks. His shirt is untucked and his black hair is messy and perfect.

I look down. I still look pretty official. Everyone else is in street clothes.

"Turn," he says. I obey, and he reaches down, unfastens my cummerbund and hands it to me. "Don't lose it," he warns. "Rico's an asshole about replacing these."

"Thanks." I smile at him.

"Although you could afford it now," he says. "Big winner. You surprised everyone."

"Yeah, well . . ." I don't know what else to say. I shouldn't have come here without some good lies in tow.

"Gonna buy me something nice?" he asks. I know he's kidding, but somehow the words are hard to hear. I can't tell him. Or anyone.

Not yet.

"Sure," I say. "Hey, um, I think I forgot something at the restaurant."

His face falls. "Oh. Okay. Want me to walk back with you?"

I shake my head. "No. It's close enough. Hold my beer. I'll be right back, okay?" I hand him the bottle. "Is there other hard alcohol here? Like tequila? We can do shots when I come back."

"Naturally," Peter says. "We'll raid the bar in the boat for the good stuff." He jerks his thumb back at the houseboat.

"Awesome. Find some Jose and wait for me, okay?"

"Anything for you, Isa," Peter says, winking.

As I walk away, I give him a little wave.

I'm not coming back.

I can't.

Finn
Sunday

Elaine Carpenter kisses me hard—harder than I've ever been kissed. Her fingers drag through my hair and pull at my clothes. She pushes me down onto the seat near the stern. The boat is empty now, clean of the litter from the party two nights before, and we're floating in the bay, too far from shore for anyone to see us.

"You're mine," she whispers, and bites my earlobe.

I pull her away so I can see her. Look in her eyes. "It's the other way around," I tell her, and she smiles at me, soft and slow. I pull her in and kiss her again, lightly. Teasingly. I know she likes this. She nips at my bottom lip and I pull away. She pouts, and I kiss her again, a little harder this time, and she moans delightedly.

"Oh, Finn," she whispers. "I love you."

I stop.

Elaine Carpenter loves me.

How weird. I always thought that the first time someone said that to me, it would be . . . different. It wouldn't be with a gorgeous 40-year-old who plays bridge with my mother every other Friday. It would be—I don't know—legal.

"What?" she whispers. She's hurt by my lack of response.

"I—I love you too, Elaine." The words sound true in my ears, and I do sort of love her. I've known her since I was little, when I used to play with her nephew, Granger, in the sandbox, and she brought us chocolate chip cookies with walnuts. And when Granger and I played football together in middle school and she brought us chocolate chip cookies with walnuts during practice.

She buries her head in my chest and I wrap her in my arms. I kiss her again, but she hardly responds. Instead, she sits up and buries her head in her hands.

"What's wrong?" I ask. I smooth her hair down. A few threads of gray show at her roots.

"I—I can't help it, Finn. I don't want you seeing anyone else. I want you all to myself."

"Do you think I'll love you less because of the others?" I ask. I try to keep my voice level. Elaine knew what she signed up for with me.

She sits up straighter, her eyes on mine. "If you loved me like I loved you, it would tear you apart to see anyone else."

I look away, out to the water, at a junky old sailboat in the distance. "I—I'm not ready for that yet."

She pouts. "What if I—"

I know what she's about to offer, and I cut her short. "No."

She pulls her robe tight around her body, like she's trying to protect herself. "Oh. Okay."

I pull her to my chest. "Come on, Elaine. Don't spoil it. We still have some time before we go back to real life."

The sailboat floats a little closer. Maybe too close. I kiss

Elaine's hair and release her—and I realize the people on the boat are waving.

They know me. Or my grandpa. Shit.

"Visitors," I say, my voice low, and Elaine perks up, her eyes wide.

"Who is it?" she asks.

I wave back. It'll seem weird if I'm unfriendly. "No idea," I tell her. "Go get dressed."

She disappears into the cabin, and I recognize the two in the distance—Aida and Jeremiah. Fuck. Did they see anything? Shit, shit, shit.

"Hey!" Aida shouts when their boat gets close enough. "What are you up to?"

"Uh, just a nice ride!" I yell back. "My grandpa asked me to take out my uncle's girlfriend! Show her the water!"

Right on cue, Elaine comes out of the cabin, wearing a wide hat and a sundress.

A very sexy, very short sundress.

"Hi," she calls across the water, giving Aida and Jeremiah a kittenish little wave.

Jeremiah's jaw drops slightly, and Aida glares. "Milf!" Jeremiah declares, and Elaine giggles, her hand on her lips.

"Aren't you cute!" she calls out to him.

Aida gives her laser eyes. "Excuse me?" she asks. Her long sundress flaps around her ankles, and her hair is free and tangled in the wind. Her arm grips Jeremiah's hand like an iron cuff.

Jeremiah puts an arm around her waist, like he just remembered she was there. "Tell your uncle I said good job!" He flashes me a thumbs-up as his sailboat passes. Once they're out of talking distance, Aida pushes Jeremiah. Their boat takes them farther into the distance, until I can barely see them.

"Shit, that was close," I say. "I don't think they saw anything, though."

Elaine presses herself against me. "That was exciting, wasn't it?" she purrs.

I step back. "If anyone actually finds out we're together, you're in huge trouble. Don't you get it? I'm seventeen!"

She puts her hands on her hips. "You aren't exactly innocent in this, you know." Her voice sours around the edges.

Ugh. I have to stop this. Have to keep her happy with our arrangement.

"Come here," I say, and she does, willingly. Easily. "I'm just looking out for you. I mean, I'm a minor. What's the worst that could happen to me? It's you I'm worried about, baby."

Elaine cuddles up against me. "You're sweet. I'm going to keep you." Her fingers touch the hem of her dress and pull it up slightly, but it doesn't interest me.

I look out at the water. In the far distance, the Waterside Café is an ant squatting on the shoreline, and for some reason, I think of Isa. Isa and her perfect ponytails and her complete and utter rejection of me.

And for one strange second, I wish that Isa were in my arms instead of Elaine.

Xavi
Wednesday

"Thanks for coming in, Xavi," Rico says. He kicks his shiny shoes up on his desk. One of his soles has a flattened slab of pink gum attached to it. Ew.

"Uh, you're welcome."

Rico puts his hands behind his head, like a bad business executive in a terrible movie. I'm not sure if he's going for intimidating or powerful, because all he's getting from me is confused. I get a hipster urge to Instagram the bottom of his shoe, but I suppress it.

"I wanted to talk to you about a financial opportunity. Would you be interested in that?"

I sit very straight. "Yes. I would be very interested in that. Are you, um, referring to a waitressing job?"

I try to sound super professional, like how I would sound if I was interviewing for a job in New York City at, like, a fashion magazine, or maybe for some sort of amazing designer. Like, maybe I am actually interviewing with Marc Jacobs. *The* actual Marc Jacobs.

I would definitely be wearing stilettos. And I would have a much better outfit. Also, my hair would not be in a tight bun.

"Not exactly. But it will lead to a waitressing job."

I frown. Um, come again? "So—what is it, exactly?"

"A time-honored tradition among the most . . . admirable of my employees. A secret, between us. And something that will allow you to buy into Tips tomorrow evening."

I grip the bottom of my chair. I have a strange, sour taste in my mouth. I swallow hard. "I'm listening."

"All you'd need to do is what many, many girls before you have done. Show me a . . . picture. A sort of burlesque photo, if you will. No clothes. Something tasteful, of course." He licks his lips.

I stare at Rico. I can feel my pulse in my head. "A . . . a naked picture? You want me to give you a naked picture?"

He nods. "Nothing digital. A Polaroid, for example. And you have my word no one will ever see the photo beyond me."

My stomach twists. "I can't give you a picture like that." I don't even like to see myself naked. I definitely don't want proof of my nakedness lying in Rico's drawer somewhere. *Rico.* Ew.

Peter was right. He doesn't want to promote me because I did a good job or because I really need this. He wants to get off.

That's all.

And he wants to use me to do it.

A dull ache starts deep in my chest. "Naked pictures?" I say again. "For real?" I touch the cigarette I've tucked behind my ear.

"I'm very serious." He finally takes his feet off the desk and leans forward, folding his hands. "Many of my waitresses do it."

"They do?" I stare behind him, at the clock on the wall. The methodical ticking is almost louder than the blood in

71

my ears. The ticking matches up with my pulse.

"Yes. About fifteen, so far. Think of it," he says, "as a dare, between us. A dare that will allow you to buy into Tips for the rest of the summer and get you a waitressing role before you turn seventeen. You'll have more money that you know what do you with. More than you've ever had."

Design school.

The money could get me into fashion design school. It could get me everything I ever wanted. I could leave this horrible place. I could leave my lovesick mother and stepfather and Peter. Maybe I could do boarding school in New York City until I graduate, and maybe I could get an internship somewhere. An internship with a *designer*.

All at the price of my dignity. But who *hasn't* taken naked photos? Like, every celebrity does it. And then I am pretty sure they secretly arrange to have naked photos released for publicity, so it's not even like a scandal anymore. It's just like a thing people do for attention.

But . . .

"You'd pay me into Tips for the whole summer? And I could keep the money if I won? And you'd never show anyone—ever?"

Rico holds up a finger. "Don't forget you'd be a waitress. And you'd be getting real tips. Which you would keep. It would be a major step up for you, Xavi. And I'd throw in your choice of shifts, of course. No slow morning shifts, unless you want to work brunch."

My heart starts beating like a jackrabbit's. I don't like him. I don't like the way my name sounds in his mouth. It's too slippery.

It's wrong.

It's all wrong.

But I want everything he's offering.

"A dare," I say. I do dares all the time. I'm good at them. But . . .

He smiles. "Yes. A dare. A dare that's just between us." He points at me, and then back at himself.

Could I do it? Could I use money I got from selling my body to—a thirtysomething creeperfest?

I imagine my first day at design school. Sitting down at the drawing board. Would I be thinking about the clothes I was about to design or—

Or what I'd done to get there?

Could I really do my best work I if were a huge whore? Or would I segue into designing leather bustiers and fuzzy handcuffs?

I've heard that the ends justify the means or whatevs, but these are some pretty intense means.

"What do you say, Xavi?" Rico says. He drums his fingers on the desk.

I swallow hard. "No."

I know it's right, but it still hurts to say it.

The hope drops off his face. "No?"

I shake my head and look at him, right in his stupid eyes. "I can't do that. I'd rather earn a waitressing job because I'm good. Not because you've seen my—" I cut off, and hover my hand over my chest.

"No one would know," Rico says gently. "You have my word on that."

I want to cry. There is a thick feeling in my throat and my

eyes burn. I stand, blinking hard. I will not cry in front of him. But this is all worse than a real dare. This isn't something fun and crazy you do in front of your friends. This isn't like the drunk striptease Aida did last year. This is something else altogether.

"No."

Rico grins at me. "You'll change your mind. Just know that the offer stands."

I drop my gaze. I can't stand to look at him. I turn away.

"I guess you weren't as interested in your future as I thought."

I force myself to look back at him. "I guess you're a sexist assface."

I slam his office door on my way out.

Peter
Thursday

Clark Hamilton, a reporter from the *Turner Gazette*, snaps a picture of me. "This is going to be sensational," he says. "I can see it. The chef behind Dubois. You'll have your choice of jobs—any restaurant in the state. Maybe the region. Wherever you want. All yours." He takes another picture. Shit. That flash is bright. I blink hard. "This article is going to change your life."

I pause from stirring a southern-style banana pudding. This newspaper guy is really oversensationalizing me. This was supposed to be a puff piece. Not a groundbreaking journalism story. The way this guy is going on, you'd think a Pulitzer was on the line and I was going to skyrocket to stardom because I was featured in a half-page article in a regional newspaper. "These are really Chef Dubois's recipes, you know. I just put them together. It's not like I'm this insane culinary genius."

"So Chef Dubois is insane?"

What is he talking about? "Of course not. It's an expression."

I glance at Rico, who is pacing around the kitchen, holding

his chin, listening to every word I say, dictator style—nodding at the stuff he agrees with and shaking his head at the stuff he doesn't. I know he wants the article to be about him, and any other day, I'd throw him a bone or an opportunity to talk to the reporter, at least. But I've half hated him since Xavi told me he's offering her some sort of opportunity. I don't trust him.

If the reporter decides he needs some Rico in his story, fine. But I'm not giving it to him. I won't even acknowledge he's here.

"What else is on the menu for this evening?"

"Everything," I tell him. "For one of the specials tonight, I'm going to be preparing chicken Dijon in a really nice sauce. Sometimes I add just a pinch of my own seasoning for an extra pop. The customers really seem to like it. Oh, and I'll do a chicken liver pâté tomorrow. For dessert, Dubois has the most incredible recipe for *tartes tatin*. It will blow your mind."

Mr. Hamilton chuckles. "Banana pudding and *tartes tatin*? What an interesting combination." He pulls a tiny pad from his pocket and scribbles something.

"Well, Chef Dubois likes to keep things interesting." I begin arranging the pudding on the little serving dishes. No Nilla wafers here—just a dollop of rich cream. I slide him a small bowl. "Here. Try it."

Mr. Hamilton grabs a heaping spoonful and devours it. He pauses thoughtfully. "Not bad. Actually, very good. And I'm a self-professed hater of banana pudding since my grandmother accidentally dropped a cat in hers."

"Um. A cat?" This guy is weird.

He waves away my question. "Long story for another time." He taps his pen against his lips. A small smudge of pudding is trapped on his goatee. I hand him a napkin, and he does this weird dabbing thing at his lips, completely missing the mess.

"Now," Mr. Hamilton says, leaning over the counter. He casts a glance back at Rico, who is still pacing back and forth. "Did you say you use a seasoning of your creation? Something that Chef Dubois did *not* create himself?"

"Sure," I say. "I do it with a few of the dishes. Our patrons here have different preferences, you know? You can't just make the same thing all the time. It'd be boring. We might lose people."

"And what is in these seasonings?"

"State secrets, mostly." I laugh. Rico stops pacing and glares at me.

"Something to add?" I call back to him, breaking my vow not to talk to the guy. "I mean, you look like you have something to say."

It comes out a lot more smartass than I mean it to. But then I don't care.

Mr. Hamilton doesn't even turn to look at Rico. "So—what's your secret, then?"

"The people here, I guess." Rico stops looking quite so angry. "The waitstaff, I mean. The employees. They're all pretty cool. Xavi, one of our busgirls, is just great. Our customers love her, even though she doesn't have a lot of contact with them. One of our waiters—Finn—is a huge draw. He's just amazing with people. They flock to him. Celia, the dishwasher, keeps everything going smoothly behind the scenes. No one gets how important that is. Everyone's just a good team here, you know?"

Mr. Hamilton nods. And for the very first time, he turns back to Rico. "You manage here, correct?"

Rico nods. "I am the manager, yes." His chest puffs out a little bit.

"What do you say to allegations that your restaurant is— ah—not exactly thriving despite the business you do?"

Rico's eyes go wide, and he stutters a little before he answers. "Uh. Uh. I guess—we could always use more business but—look at the people coming through the doors—uh—"

"I see." Mr. Hamilton cuts him short. "Well, that's really all I need here. Peter, thank you so much for letting me back here to see you at work." He winks. "I'm a bit of a foodie, so I really can't wait for this piece to run. I think it'll be big for you. You'll see." He sticks out his hand, and I wipe my hands off on my apron before taking it.

"Thank you, Mr. Hamilton," I say. "If you have any other questions or anything, you can call me. I'm sure Rico won't mind. I think you'll see we're a fine, upstanding establishment."

I shouldn't bait Rico. His shoulders move up and down in his expensive suit, like he's breathing too hard.

"Thank you, Peter. Watch for this in next week's issue, okay?"

I nod, and he leaves through the back door. Rico watches him go, and then rounds on me, his mouth fixed in a hard line.

"Why did you tell him you change Dubois's recipes?" he says, putting his hands on his head. "Why would you do that in the first place, Peter? They don't come here for your food! They come here for Dubois!"

Huh. Suddenly, he's singing a different tune. Hadn't he just said I was ready to take Dubois's place?

"I didn't think it was a big deal." I finish the banana

puddings and start covering them and lining them up in the fridge. They'll all be gone in the next of couple hours anyway, but it's better to be safe.

Rico slams his hand on the silver scale squatting on the counter. "Peter, you are *not* the story here. Chef Dubois is the story. He always has been, and he's why we are successful. And from now on, you *will* stick to his recipes. Is that clear?"

I slam the refrigerator shut and stare at him. I want to take my apron off and throw it on the floor. Spit at him. Quit.

Chef Dubois is never here, anyway.

But I can't. If I don't watch out for Xavi—God knows what Rico will do. God knows what he's already asked of her. I can't leave her alone. Not with him as a boss.

So I smile at him.

"Sure. Sorry about that."

Xavi bursts into the kitchen suddenly, her usually perfect hair coming undone. Her makeup is smudged. Like she's been crying.

"Xavi," I say, forgetting Mr. Hamilton and Rico. "You okay?"

She ducks her head so I can't see her face, and hurries toward the staff bathroom. Her shirt is untucked in the back. Rico glances at her. "Leave her alone," he says. "You have work to do."

I glare at him. "She's my stepsister, dude."

Rico crosses his arms. "Yeah, I know. Now, can I have some of that banana pudding?"

I want to kill him.

"Lick the bowl," I say, and stalk out the back door for some fresh air.

Isa
Friday

"Isa?" Finn asks, peeking into the kitchen. "There's a couple out front asking for you." He jerks his thumb over his shoulder, motioning toward the floor.

"For me?" I ask. "Are you sure they aren't confused? You're the one who gets all of the requests."

"For you." He smiles. "You're getting a clientele."

I finish washing my hands. I'd just finished snacking on these insanely delicious strawberry-turtle cheesecake circles that Peter had been testing out. That guy is a culinary van Gogh. No joke.

"I can't think of anyone who would like me enough to request me," I say, shaking the excess water off my hands and grabbing a paper towel.

"I would."

I catch Finn's eyes in the mirror. They're definitely serious. And sultry.

But definitely serious.

"Um, thanks." I flash him a quick beauty-queen smile—practiced and easy and totally genuine . . . at least, to anyone who isn't used to me in a sparkly dress and a tiara. "But other than the Witch, I don't have any big fans."

"Go check it out," Finn urges.

I straighten my shirt and walk out onto the floor to see who has requested me.

And I've definitely seen them before.

But not often.

My parents.

My mother stands and waves excitedly, the fringe on her shirt bouncing with the movement. My dad's face stretches into a grin. His beard is somehow less salt-and-pepper than I'd remembered.

They look great—young and rested and totally stress-free. Not like you'd expect parents to look. My mother wears heavy black eyeliner and my father's haircut is more what you'd expect on Kurt Cobain.

When they'd actually been at home, they'd looked like parents. My dad wore suits to work and my mom wore elastic jeans. They were completely dorky—and normal. But since they set out to make it as rock gods . . . well . . . a little less parental. A little opening up the family album to find white powder between the pages, if you know what I mean.

Yep. My parents are cool.

And it. Totally. Sucks.

My great-aunt must have told them I worked here. I haven't talked to them since the beginning of the summer. Before I even started.

"Hey, sweetie!" Mom says. She grabs my wrists and looks at me for a second, beaming, and then wraps me into a hug. I hug her back hesitantly. She feels too skinny.

"Hey, Mom."

I glance up at my dad, who is smiling at me, his hands in his pockets. "Come here, honey," he says. He hugs me tightly. "You look beautiful."

I smile at them. I can't help it, no matter how much I hate them sometimes. "I'm glad you guys are here. Do you want to eat, or are you just dropping in?"

"No," Dad declares, grinning. "We want to eat. We want to see your fine waitressing skills at work."

"Okay, then. Ah, drinks?"

My parents never turn down alcohol.

"The Bordeaux," Mom says. "For both of us."

I nod. "I'll be right back."

I hit up the bar, where Peter is pouring. Josh, the cook who works when Peter isn't around, is getting some extra experience in the kitchens, since Rico doesn't think he's quite up to snuff—or at least, not nearly as good as Peter. So Peter's letting Josh handle lunchtime while he's still in the restaurant, in case Josh needs any pointers. Peter's technically not old enough to be a bartender, but I'm not exactly old enough to serve, either. The cops who get cheap drinks don't seem too bothered.

"Two glasses of Bordeaux." I smile at Peter.

"Who are they?" Peter asks, nodding toward my parents. "Wait—are they Ambient Two?"

I blush. "Um, yeah. That's them."

"No. Way. They are tearing up the indie scene." He leans over the bar to get a better look at them. "You are so lucky you got their table."

I sniff. "Sure. So, *so* lucky." Of course, tearing up the indie scene doesn't actually mean making money, the way they do it. Not with the drugs, the alcohol, and the clothes that cost more than twice the rent of our trailer.

"That is *sick*," Peter reaches out for a fist bump. I ignore his outstretched hand.

"They're my parents, Peter."

"Uh. Come again? They're, like, thirty."

I shake my head. "No, they aren't. They're my mom and dad. They don't come around much. I live with my great-aunt while they tour."

Why am I telling him this? I've spent most of my time pretending that they don't exist. That I don't have a connection with them. That they aren't the reason I'm living in redneckville with my great-aunt. I should fake like I don't know them.

"Oh," he says. "I get it."

I'm not sure if he does, but to his credit, he pours the wine quietly and hands the glasses to me without a sympathetic smile attached.

"Tips tomorrow?" he asks instead.

"Obviously." I smile at him to show him I'm grateful, and take the Bordeaux back to my parents, who are dragging their fingers over the menus, trying to sound out the French names in ridiculous accents.

"Uh, what do you recommend, sweetie?" Dad asks, glancing up at me. "I'm not familiar with a lot of this."

I take a glance at the menu. It changes a little from day to day. "What about one of our specials? The *moules marinière* are really good."

Mom shoots me a blank look. "Moles?"

"Mussels," I explain. "And the chocolate éclairs are delicious, if you're thinking dessert."

"We'll have . . . that. Both of those things," Mom says. She hands me back the menu. "You look different, Isa."

"I do?" I ask.

"Yeah," she says, studying me, her eyes flicking up and down.

Of course I do. My mom prefers me done up in pageant wear. She'd be perfectly happy if I were in false eyelashes and glitter every day of the week. And when she lived with us, I was. But that stuff is annoying, not to mention expensive. And guys like me better without hair extensions and twelve layers of foundation. If I'd kissed Finn in that mess, he'd have come away looking like he made out with a rodeo clown.

A couple of other customers come in. Finn plays host—Rico really, really needs to hire one—and seats them. I move away from my parents' table.

"Wait," Dad says. "Aren't you going to hang out with us?" He motions at an empty chair.

"Dad, I'm working," I say. "Let me put your order in to the kitchen and take care of my other tables. I'll be right back, okay?"

He sighs heavily. "Okay, Isa." But as I walk away, he shakes his head at my mother.

They don't get it.

At least their food shouldn't take long—Josh is cooking up loads of the specials. It's easier that way, and Josh is super paranoid about getting behind. But we stall, generally, lest the customers think their meals have been sitting out. Which I guess they have.

I put the order in and run into Finn. "Are you okay?" he asks. "You seem . . . off."

I want to be offended, but what's the point? I square my shoulders and tighten my hair tie. "Yeah, I'm fine."

I feel my parents' eyes on me while I take orders and fetch drinks for the other tables. I decide to go grab their food now instead of making them wait. The sooner they leave, the easier the day will be for me. I help Josh fix up their plates quickly and carry them out with all the grandeur I can muster.

They only want the best.

"This is just beautiful, Isa," Mom says, clasping her hands together. "We need to come here more often, don't we, Chad?" She grins at my father.

"Definitely." Dad digs in with his fork. "We have a gig tomorrow two towns over. You should really come," he says around a mouthful of food.

"Yeah," I say. "That would be great. I'd like that."

But tomorrow is Tips.

I won't come.

Even if I didn't have cash riding on a good dare.

"Are you doing more pageants, honey?" Mom asks. "Did you sign up for the Miss Teen Moonshine?"

"Sure, Mom." It won't hurt her to think that I did. But Miss Teen Moonshine was last month, and I spent it watching reruns of *Jeopardy!* at home while some other girl paraded around to win a sparkly crown and a souvenir moonshine jug. Mom won't check up on me anyway.

An elderly man a few tables away motions me over and asks for his steak to be returned to the kitchen and cooked properly.

"I'll be right back," I mouth at my parents while I carry his food back to the kitchen and put in my parents' order for the chocolate éclairs. Finn catches me again.

"Can you watch table seven for a half second?" he asks. "I'm getting slammed."

"Sure," I say. I smile at him. I'm grateful for another distraction. Grateful for a reason for less awkward conversation. For less sadness and pressure.

But when I return to the floor, my parents' table is empty. Half-eaten plates of mussels are abandoned, but all of the wine is gone. They didn't stick around to even try the chocolate éclairs.

Or pay their bill.

There's a note scribbled on the white cloth napkin.

Love you, sweetie! Pls take care of meal with discount. Pay you back later.

The bill is $150.

My discount is 10 percent.

I wish they'd never come.

Finn
Saturday

I can't think straight. Everything in my head is a fucking mess.

Maybe I should call in sick. Maybe I should just abandon the whole idea.

But I'm not used to this. I'm not sure how Peter does it every single day.

"Did you hear me, young man?" Anastasia Parker snaps her fingers at me. One of her fake fingernails falls off and bounces beneath the table.

"You ordered the soufflé," I say. "And a glass of our finest champagne?"

She scowls at me and pets the fur wrap she wears year round—even in the hottest days of summer. "Smarter than you look, aren't you?"

No. That's one thing I never got: the smarts. Looks and talent on the football field can only get a guy so far, and then it's swinging a hammer on some construction site for the rest of my life until I get too old to do it anymore. I'm not one of those dumb jocks reveling in his glory years.

I'm one of those dumb jocks watching the best part of my

life come to a close. And the worst part is, I know it. I feel every day slipping away from me.

I flash her a quick smile and put her order in to the kitchen. "Anything for you, Mrs. Parker."

She scowls at me. Her hooded eyes narrow to tiny little slits.

There's no way in hell she can see like that.

I even scrunch my eyes up on the way to the kitchens to see if I can see.

I can't.

"What are you doing?"

I open my eyes. Isa is staring at me, her hands perched on her hips. "Uh. Trying to see if I could, you know. See. Like, with my eyes shut like that."

"What?" Isa frowns at me. A piece of hair has escaped from her careful bun.

"Have you ever waited on Anastasia Parker?" I ask.

"Oh, the old chick with the fox fur stole?" Isa asks with a grin. "Super heinous? Always orders 'the finest glass of champagne'?" She makes finger quotes.

I make the Anastasia eyes at her. "You know how she sort of crumples up her whole face and glares at you?"

Isa stares at me for a minute, then cracks up. "Yes!" She imitates the face. "She's worse than the Witch at table twelve! She's so *mean!*"

"The Witch loves you," I say. "And she hates all girls! Something's wrong with you."

Isa hits me on the arm. "Finn!" She laughs. "Maybe I'm just a good waitress!"

"Whatever you want to believe, Isa." I smile at her to let her know I'm joking.

Wow. I'm actually having a friendly conversation with Isa. Maybe even flirting. It's not even that hard. Only . . . I feel a line of sweat form on my upper lip. And my palms feel weird. Tingly.

Maybe this isn't right.

Isa purses her lips. "Finn, are you okay? Do you need to go sit down? Your color's a little funny."

"I'm fine," I say. "I need to get Anastasia Parker's order in to the kitchen."

I hurry past her, ducking my head slightly, like that'll actually help. But *fuck*. I can hook up with Elaine like it's my job and I can't even ask Isa for her phone number?

Something is wrong with me. I need a head doctor. I think I'm crazy. I can see it now, all over the local newspapers: *Quarterback Admitted to Insane Asylum.*

Or maybe a mental hospital. Or wherever it is that crazy people go now. And the worst part is, I don't even like Isa. Or maybe I do. I guess—I guess I'm not exactly sure.

I turn in my order to Josh, the frazzled cook working the lunch rush today. His nose twitches when he's stressed, and he looks like a damned rabbit right now. Looking at him calms me down, as weird as it is.

At least I'm not Josh.

"Why you going all Peter Cottontail, man?" I ask. I tear the top sheet off my pad and clip it up for him where he can see it.

He wrinkles his nose. "These orders. I can't keep up. I'm not a cook. I'm like, a cook's assistant who is about to burn this mother down." He slams a skillet down and pushes his black-framed glasses up his nose.

I shake my head. Josh always gets really weird when he's stressed out. Which is every day he comes to work. Dude is high-strung. He smokes too much weed and gets paranoid, and he always thinks that the government is tapping his cell phone, when we all know the government is tapping *everyone's* cell phones.

It's not like he's special.

"Oh shit, oh shit, where are the green apples, Finn? I lost the green apples!"

I pick them up off the scale. "Here, dude. They're right here. Pull yourself together, man. The lunch is just getting started."

"Go get Peter," he says. "Bring him in here. I need him."

Celia appears in the kitchen, her red hair huge and frizzed from the humid air around the dishwasher. "Josh, dude. Pull. It. Together. Finn is not going to get Peter. You're going to stop and do some calm, deep breathing and handle this."

Josh leans against the side of the sink and breathes, very deeply. Celia flashes me the thumbs-up and mouths, "Go. Now."

I nod and escape the kitchen. I snag the priciest champagne from Peter (although I bet him fifty bucks that Mrs. Parker wouldn't notice if we gave her the cheapest shit we have) and head back to Anastasia's table, where I present her with the flute.

She tries to smile at me. Her lipstick is smeared up the side of her cheek. It wasn't like that a few months ago. She sniffs her champagne. "Now, Finn—it is Finn, isn't it?"

"Yes, ma'am," I say.

"My friend Marjorie heard from her friend Bernard you have a little side business. Is that true?" She folds her hands and rests her chin delicately on them, something of a smile playing around the sides of her drooping mouth.

Oh, dear God, no. Not Anastasia Parker. Anyone but Anastasia Parker.

I scratch my head. "Um, what?"

"What if I were to express an interest in this business of yours?"

I don't meet her eyes. "Uh. Like, as an investor?"

She can't mean what I think she means. She can't. There's no way.

She leans forward, gripping the top of her tall steel cane. She reeks of old lady perfume. Like flowers and bacon grease. "As a customer. Finn, I want to play."

"I'm—ah—I'm not taking on new clients right now, Mrs. Parker."

She winks at me and a bit of glitter falls off her wrinkled eye. "Look at my tip and then we'll talk."

"It—it's okay, Mrs. Parker. Don't leave me a big tip. I mean—I don't have time, and football is starting up."

She scowls again, very suddenly. "Go get my soufflé. I'm tired as hell of waiting on you."

I nod and turn quickly, stalking toward the kitchen. I am done. I am so done. No more side business. No more money. I don't care.

Isa catches me on my way to the back patio. "Hey, Finn," she says. "What's up with you today?"

I shake my head and laugh. Life is a funny, stupid thing.

"Nothing," I say. "Hey—can I get your number? We should hang out sometime. Outside of work, I mean. It could be cool."

Isa tosses her head back and studies me for a minute. "Yeah, sure, Finn." She pulls up the sleeve of my white shirt, grabs a pen from her apron, and writes her digits carefully along my wrist. "Call me?"

I grin. "Yeah. Of course."

What do you know? Something went right today.

This is progress.

Xavi
Sunday
3:00 a.m.

"Did you hear, dude?" Warren tells Jake. "That super old chick who comes into the restaurant all the time—Anastasia Parker—gave Finn a four-hundred dollar tip. Four. Hundred. Bucks. That's *insane*."

Jake laughs. "He must have slipped her more than just food."

Ugh. Guys are so gross. Anastasia Parker is, like, eight hundred years old and wears a decrepit old fur that smells like mothballs. I ignore the boys and settle into a lawn chair on the roof, my scrapbook hugged tightly to my chest. Tips is happening, but I didn't buy in tonight. I couldn't afford it. And I couldn't—well, you know. Expose my Playboy parts for a shot at the big time.

Still, sitting on the roof, watching all of the players drinking . . . I wish I had.

Well, almost.

There's still a part of me that's pretty proud I didn't ditch my rags for an old dude. But I'm pretty sure that part of me is my mom.

I look around the circle. Aida hasn't bought in either. At

least, I don't think so, judging by her expression. The way she's sitting away from everyone. The way she doesn't talk or laugh or join the circle. She's not even close to Jeremiah, which is weird. I thought he'd have to get her surgically removed before she voluntarily gave up burrowing into his side like a tick.

The roof door flops open and Rico climbs out of the hatch, a twenty-four-pack of beer in his hand. "Ready to play?" he asks.

Everyone cheers loudly.

I sneer at him, and a heavy feeling settles its way into my heart. This totally had to be how Leonardo DiCaprio felt when he lost the Oscar for the billionth time. Or how LaRina Hughes felt last year, when she turned down the opportunity to cheat on her history exam . . . and lost valedictorian to Tori McEntire, who totally cheated.

I rest my scrapbook on my lap. I don't have to open it to know every page by heart. It's everything I want. Perfect outfits, designed and drawn to perfection by yours truly. Sky-high heels with delicate buckles and adorable peep-toe ballet flats and big, full skirts and mermaid dresses. Everything I've ever imagined.

And a scant few blank pages in the back where I haven't drawn anything. Yet.

The cover is brown and worn. Small cracks inch their way up the leather. It looks older than it is, faded from too much handling and years of living in my backpack, crushed with heavy textbooks and loose pencils and old scraps of spiral-notebook paper.

Maybe it's weird that I brought it here, but I needed it with me. I needed to remind myself why I didn't do it.

Or why I should.

"Xavi!" Rico shouts. "Last minute entry?" He smiles crookedly at me.

I shake my head. "No." I hate the word and I hate myself and I hate Rico. Because I want in. I want to play.

I want fashion school.

Rico shrugs and turns his back to me. He pops open a Miller Lite and takes a huge drink. "Tonight," he says, "Warren with the dare!"

Celia reaches over and hits play on her iPod. Eye of the Tiger blares from the speakers and Warren does a lap around the roof, fists in the air. Everyone cheers and hoots. Finn follows him around the roof, pretending to hold some sort of torch.

"All the normal rules apply," Rico reminds everyone. "So. Warren. I gave you some time to think on it. What's your dare?"

It's funny. You never know when Rico is going to tap you for a dare. You might have the full two weeks—or you might have two minutes.

Warren sits down near the fire and does a drumroll on his chair, a grin on his square face. "Dare participants?"

Isa stands first, grinning proudly, followed by Finn. My stepbrother pushes out of his chair, and Jake. Next Jeremiah, Aida, and Josh. I guess Aida's in after all.

And then Celia. Celia. She stands and prances over to Rico. She stuffs a thick fold of bills into his hands. She drops one—a twenty—and it lands on Rico's shoe.

Oh my gosh. Even Celia's bought in.

I'm the only one sitting. The only one not playing.

The only one out.

I glance over at Rico. He's *watching* me. Watching with a slimy, leery grin. Ugh. If this restaurant thing falls through for him, he has a bright future on *To Catch a Predator*.

"Warren, the floor's yours," Rico says, and Celia clicks off the music. Everyone stands sort of awkwardly and Warren looks from face to face. He's drawing it out. Enjoying it. Worse than Ryan Seacrest on *American Idol*.

He kind of looks like Ryan Seacrest, come to think of it. Only not miniature.

He steeples his fingers. "This dare requires—a special wardrobe." He grins. "A wardrobe assigned by me. You will have to complete this dare in the next two weeks."

"What's the dare already?" Jake asks. "Seriously, man. Stop drawing it out."

Warren raises his eyebrows. "All in good time, dude. Calm down." He pauses and digs into his left pocket, and comes out with a couple of little scraps of fabric. He spreads them out on the palm of his hand. It's a bikini. An itsy-bitsy bikini. A bikini you need a microscope to see. "Ladies!" he says. "This is your work uniform. You will wear this for an entire shift, or until a customer complains."

Jake raises his hand. "I won't complain!"

I snicker. I can't help it. Although I'd totally wear that to win Tips. Better that than naked.

"And for the menfolk," Warren says, "this little number."

He stretches the costume out on either of his thumbs.

It's a hammock.

A banana hammock.

A men's thong.

I glance at Peter's face. His eyes are wide and his skin is pale. He looks like he might toss his cookies.

I die laughing. Or, you know, the equivalent. I laugh until

it hurts deep in my stomach. Sure, I'd rather be playing. But watching is golden. "Warren," I say, "you're a genius!"

Warren smirks. "Right?"

And then I look at Rico. Occasionally, he gets a little concerned about work dares, but he seems cool with this, I guess. He's probably hoping some girl will win the dare. Rico claps his hands. "Okay. Who's out?"

Everyone exchanges glances with each other.

Celia dances back and forth, shifting her weight from one foot to the other. But she doesn't sit down. Neither does anyone else.

Peter swallows hard, and I see his Adam's apple shift slightly. He doesn't want to do this. But he doesn't move.

Holy shit. This *never happens*. But apparently everyone is cool with gallivanting about in their skivvies in front of the community's richest patrons, which occasionally includes our parents.

I mean. Not that I wouldn't do it.

"All right," Rico says. "Cash entries." He grabs the baseball cap off Warren's head. Everyone else fishes around for loose bills in their pockets. They each write their names on their bills and crush them into little green balls between their palms.

"Xavi, come help," Rico says. He smiles at me, only he does it really weird—like he knows how hard this is for me. He knows how much I want it. I just hope he knows how much I hate him right now.

I grab the baseball hat and collect bills in the hat—first Peter, then Celia, then Finn, Jeremiah, Jake, Josh, Aida, and finally Isa, who looks at me hopefully and fidgets. She seems nervous. Too nervous for someone who just won Tips. With the cash she pulled last time, she could finance Tips games for the rest of the summer. Unless she's spent it already. Unless she needs more for a reason.

Hmm. Is Isa up to something?

"I'm going to draw," Rico announces, reaching toward me, but I turn my back to him.

"I think Warren should do it. Since he made up the dare and all."

Warren wraps an arm around my waist and pulls me close to him. I giggle. "And I think Xavi should do it. She can be my lovely lady assistant."

"Well," I say, "I'm always up for that."

Warren takes the hat and holds it above my head. He mixes the bills around and I reach up, on my tippy toes, and pluck one bill from the hat. I feel like the lottery girl on channel five.

"What does it say?" Rico stands a step back from the campfire, his arms crossed over his chest. The campfire flickers strangely across his face.

I smooth out the crumpled bill. A short name is scrawled across George Washington's face in neat, square letters.

"Finn," I announce.

"Yes!" Finn fist-bumps Warren.

Isa, for some reason, turns scarlet.

Peter
Sunday

In the entire world, there's nothing I like more than this.

I take a sip of my Coke. I haven't been too excited about moving into a house that wasn't my own, but being away from the city—away from the noise—is kind of great.

Xavi's dad—her mom's first husband, who died—left them a big old house and a lot of land—including an old shed built into a big hill. If I back up my pickup just right, I can climb onto the roof and see forever—over the groves of trees and a small creek that is dry half the time and, in the distance, if I stay here late enough, the lights of the city take over a corner of the sky. I can even see over to her neighbor's property, filled with old, rusted pieces of machinery and cars from another age.

That's where I am now—on the roof with the sun just starting to creep its way toward the top of the horizon. I feel a little like a cowboy, except I've never ridden a horse in my entire life.

I take another sip of my drink. I think of Finn. Winning Tips. I'm not even disappointed. I wasn't exactly looking forward to letting everyone see my junk. That Speedo that

Warren held up didn't leave much to the imagination. And by much, I mean anything. I'm not ashamed of my equipment, but who's just going to put it out there?

Well, if you're Finn, then you just don't care.

Still. Sucks to lose the cash, though. Of course, if Finn wusses out, then all that cash goes back into the pot.

And I can win next week.

Although—who knows what I'd have to do for it. Last year, Damon Alexi accepted a dare to do a fire-walk-type thing, and he ended up in the hospital because his little toe actually melted into his other toe and he couldn't walk for, like, a month.

In the distance, I hear an engine. A low-pitched humming. Not a car, exactly. But the sound is familiar. I turn around carefully and I see it: a red four-wheeler in the distance, winding around tall yucca plants and the occasional tree. The engine revs as it hits a small gully. The driver takes it like a champ, her blond hair spread out behind her as she rides.

Wait—that's not—it can't be.

It's Xavi.

I never expected to see her on a four-wheeler. It's like seeing Jake with an actual bar of soap or Finn, God forbid, studying.

I wave at her, and she shifts down and drives over to the edge of the little shed. She shifts into neutral and shuts the four-wheeler off. "What are you doing here?" she shouts, dismounting. She's wearing shorts and a little flannel shirt. She's missed a button just below her navel, and I can get a glimpse of her skin when she moves just right. There's no way around it—Xavi is hot. Like Leia-in-*Star Wars* slave girl hot.

I try to put my hands in my pockets and realize I'm still holding my Coke. "Hanging out, I guess. What are you doing?"

She laughs this little, breathless laugh that sounds like the tinkle of a bell above a shop door. "I needed to get out of the house. My mom and your dad, they . . ." she pauses and makes a face. She doesn't need to tell me. They're acting like horny teenagers again. Which is just dumb because old people, by choosing to become parents, immediately relinquish their rights to be either horny or teenagers.

"Right," I say.

Xavi stares sort of awkwardly for a minute, and we both try to speak at the same time.

"Well—" I start.

"Uh—"

I laugh. "You first."

She looks back at the four-wheeler. "Um. I guess I'll leave you to it."

"Why don't you come up here?" I ask.

She gives the shed a once-over. "It's probably not safe," she says. "I mean, this thing hasn't been used since my dad was little."

"It's probably not." I grin at her. I balance the can carefully on the peak of the roof, where there are a couple of flat inches, and walk slowly down toward my truck. She hoists herself onto the bed.

"Come on," I say, and reach for her hand. She gives it to me and I pull her up. She wobbles, and I steady her, my hands on her arms. "Careful."

She pauses, but doesn't pull away. Her eyes meet mine, and then flick down to her feet. "Watch your step," I warn.

I keep a hand on her arm as she walks up the roof. She straddles the divide on the other side of my cooler and looks at me. Her hair is all pushed to one side and messy from her ride.

I grab her a can of lemonade from the cooler and crack it open for her. I cross over to her side and sit down next to her—not too close, but at least there isn't a cooler separating us. She swings her leg over the roof so we're side by side.

"I see you came prepared," Xavi says, eyeing the cooler. "Nice."

I try to be cool, but a smile betrays me. "Thanks, Xavi." I hand her the drink. "For you."

"Thanks." She takes a sip. "It's beautiful out here, isn't it? It's like you can see forever."

I nod. "Yeah. I guess." But it's not what's on my mind. Especially not with Xavi sitting so close.

Xavi looks sideways at me. "If it's not for the view, why are you here?"

I set down my soda and rest my elbows on my knees. "The scenery's great and all, but mostly, uh, it's a good place to think shit out."

Xavi raises an eyebrow at me. "What the hell do you have to think out? Your life is pretty easy."

I laugh. "I have lots of shit, Xavi."

"Like what?" She reaches into her pocket and brings up a very crushed cigarette, which she tucks behind her ear.

I hesitate, and she puts her hand on my wrist. "Tell me, Peter. Please?" She blinks up at me. Fuck. She's gorgeous. And I like the way my name sounds in her mouth.

"Well. For example. Remember that newspaper article?"

She nods.

"Well, the article came out yesterday. Mr. Hamilton, the reporter—he quoted me saying I want to become a chef. Dad is pissed. He's going to make me quit the restaurant for good after the summer, or"—I pause and take a sip—"I have to move out."

Xavi's eyes go wide. "Seriously? That's ridiculous."

"Well, he didn't raise me to be a nancy-boy chef. Or so he says." I grimace and look away from Xavi, where the sun is bleeding into the horizon.

"That sucks," Xavi says. "I'm sorry."

"It's fine," I say. I'm not sure why I've just told her all of this. She probably thinks I'm being stupid. Or maybe she'll start thinking of me the way my father does.

Or worse, she'll pity me.

She sets her lemonade on the cooler. Her hand finds mine.

We sit that way for a long time, without talking—just watching the sky and the lights blink on in the city. She doesn't let go of my hand. She interlaces her fingers with mine.

Linking us together.

"Xavi?" I ask, finally.

"Yeah?" Her breath is a little short. She smells like the country air and apple cider.

I hesitate, and she nudges me with her shoulder.

"Can I—can I kiss you?"

She smiles up at me, her lips pressed together. "Okay."

I put my fingers on her chin and draw her to me. Her face tilts up and her eyes close.

Her lips are soft. She tastes like licorice.

In the entire world, there's nothing I like more than this.

Isa
Monday

I can't believe I'm doing this. I must be crazy. I have to be.

I'm going on a date with *Finn*.

Beautiful, funny, kind-of-sweet Finn, who's a great kisser. And who blushes when he talks to me. Finn, who was sweating and shaky when he asked for my number, and who is adorable and clueless and holds the door for me when we walk into the restaurant.

Finn, who insulted me when I started and has spent every single day since trying to make up for it.

He gives me a funny little smile as I walk in. "You look . . . nice," he says, taking in my purple sundress. His voice is off, like he hasn't spoken in weeks. Which, with Finn, is *so* not the case. The guy's definitely not quiet. He's nervous. To be on a date with *me*.

It's sort of nice. I haven't been on a date in six months, since Tommy Feller took me to a movie. He ended up bringing a flask into the movie theater, asked if I'd heard of the popcorn box trick (ew), and threw up on my favorite suede heels before the night was out.

But tonight is going to be different. The restaurant is

gorgeous. Not as nice as Waterside, sure, but not much is. The floor is concrete, and ornate iron tables crouch delicately beneath short white tablecloths. Wreathes hang from the ceiling. The sides of the building are open—it looks like they operate like a glass garage door of sorts. The breeze floats in, making the wreaths move slightly, and the flowers in the vases on the tables shift. Finn looks amazing, dressed in black pants and a crisp cornflower-blue button-up.

"Finn," I whisper, "it's perfect."

He smiles for real. "I thought you'd like it. It's a drive, but it's worth it."

The server seats us at a table near the street. Tiny tea lights line the sidewalk outside. It doesn't feel like we're just in another city—it feels like another world. I can't believe that Finn, of all people, decided to take me *here*.

"Want something to drink?" Finn asks, a little shyly. His cheeks are rosy. He's beautiful in a way that few people are. Perfect.

I look to my left and right, and lean across the table to whisper. "I'd order champagne, but I don't have a fake."

The corner of his mouth pulls up. "That's fine." His eyes search the room, and he motions a waiter over. "Could we order a bottle of champagne, please?"

"Certainly," the waiter says, inclining his head slightly. Finn slips him a bill, and the waiter leaves, tucking it carefully into his pocket.

I find myself holding back a smile. That's the nice thing about being on a date with a server. They're never rude to the waitstaff.

The waiter returns a moment later with a bottle of

champagne and a towel. He opens it quietly and pours us each a flute of the bubbly stuff before leaving it on ice . . . and handing me a single yellow daisy.

"From the gentleman," he says.

I glow at Finn.

"Do you like it?" he asks.

I nod. "No one's ever given me a flower before." It's weird, admitting that. No one.

"What's your favorite flower?" Finn asks me. "Did I do okay?"

"You did great." I breathe in the daisy and set it in my water glass. "Although—this is super weird, I know—but my favorite flower is a dandelion. My mom used to make bracelets for me out of the stems." Back when she was actually home. We'd blow the delicate seedlings off the fluffy ones and wear more bracelets than we could count.

Finn leans over and touches my nose. "Sorry. You had a bit of pollen. Just there." He shows me the yellow dust on his fingers, and I laugh and touch my nose. "Peter said your parents came in the other day. They're musicians, right? How cool is that?"

For a moment, I hate my parents. I hate the questions about them and how everyone thinks of me differently when they find out they front a semifamous band.

I hate that Peter told.

I nod. "Um, yes. I don't talk to them much, because they're on the road all the time, which is fine. We're not very close."

"So do you get to live by yourself? That would be sick. Think of the *parties*."

I hesitate. "I live with my great-aunt." In a trailer park.

Which he will hopefully never, ever see. I made him pick me up about two blocks away, at a park. He didn't ask why.

"That's cool," Finn says. "Do you get along with her?"

"Sure." When she looks away from her shows or isn't working. Which is almost never. In fact, I could probably throw a massive party and she wouldn't even get out of her recliner. "What about your parents?" I ask.

Finn shrugs. "My dad's my high school football coach. My mom is an interior designer. I have four older brothers who have all moved as far away as possible, and three of them are playing ball in college."

"Is that weird?" I ask. "I mean, having your dad as your coach?"

Finn shakes his head. "Not really. I mean, after four brothers I'm kind of used to it. He's not my dad at practice. He's my coach. And he doesn't give a shit what I do as long as I work hard."

"I see." I fidget in my seat. I don't want to talk about parents anymore. Is this going well? I can't tell if this is going well. The flower was nice, but if he says one more thing about my parents, I might scream. "I think I'm being awkward," I tell Finn, and then I want to hit myself in the face. Why would I say that out loud? Oh my gosh, what is wrong with me? Did I seriously just say something that stupid?

Finn picks up his flute and downs his champagne, and then pours more. "Should we get drunk?"

I shrug. I don't really want to get drunk. I think of Tommy Feller throwing up on my shoes. "No, thank you."

Finn sets his glass down slowly. "Oops," he says.

"It's whatever," I say. "I can drive home."

"That wouldn't be right," Finn says. "Anyway."

"Anyway."

We stare at each other. I check my phone.

No one has texted me. Someone has, however, posted an adorable puppy photo on my Facebook. I show Finn.

"Cute," he says.

He checks his phone.

"Um," I say. Nothing comes after.

My tongue sticks to the roof of my mouth.

This is so goddamned weird. And it started *so well*.

This is my fault. I fell off the good-date train the moment Finn asked me about my parents.

"What music do you like?" Finn asks.

Oh my gosh. Not the music questions. Are we really that far down in the proverbial social well? Is a social well even "proverbial"?

"Anything. Um, do you mind if I excuse myself for a moment?" I stand, and he stands too. He's so polite. I hurry off to the bathroom, and it's really, really hard for me not to just walk right out the emergency exit next to the bathroom door.

I stand in front of the mirror. Why can't I pull it together long enough for a fucking date? Why am I so weird? Ugh. My reflection stares back at me, the picture of a much more put-together girl. Finn probably thinks I hate him. But I don't. I like him. And everything he's done. It's sweet and kind, and nothing like anyone I've ever been with before.

I'm going to do this. I'm going to go back out there, and I'm going to tell him I don't like talking about my parents. And then we can talk about something we're both interested in. Like—uh—Tips.

Because clearly, we are both good at it.

I square my shoulders and walk back out onto the floor, where Finn is waiting at the table. The bright color of embarrassment is gone from his cheeks. I sit back down and he smiles at me.

"Sorry about all of that," I say. "I don't really like talking about my parents. Did you know they stuck me with their check when they came in?"

"It's fine," Finn says, and suddenly, I'm relieved. I don't know why I let them get to me so much. Abandonment issues, I guess. "And they sound pretty shitty," he adds.

I nod. It's sort of nice, actually, to hear someone else acknowledge it.

I have shitty parents.

"So," I say, grinning a little evilly, "when are you going to fulfill your little dare?"

He winces. "Don't say little. Ouch."

I laugh in spite of myself. "I'm sure you'll be spectacular." I turn to reach into my purse for lip gloss. "I know I'm looking forward to it."

I bend over a little farther to reach deeper into the handbag. My lip gloss must've slipped out of its pocket. And then, from out of nowhere, a hand deals me a sharp, stinging slap across the face.

I grab my cheek and look up, where a stunning woman in a silver dress is standing, her hands on her hips.

"You bitch!" she screams.

Finn

Monday

I stand up too quickly. My legs knock into the table and make the ice in the water glasses rattle. "Elaine! What the fuck?"

The whole restaurant has gone still and silent. The only sound is laughter from the kitchens, where they clearly have no idea what's going on.

She glares at me for a moment, her hands still stuck to her hips, and then a waiter approaches her. "Mrs. Carpenter?" he says, his voice very quiet. "I'm afraid I'm going to have to ask you to leave." He draws back, like he's afraid she's going to hit him, too, but Elaine just runs out of the restaurant, her high heels making loud *clomp-clomp* noises like horseshoes.

Isa's eyes are filled with tears, but I'm not sure if it's because she's upset or because Elaine really hit her.

And she did. Really hit her, I mean. That smack was *loud*. A raised red handprint is blooming over Isa's cheek. I've seen enough football injuries to know she'll probably have an angry purple bruise.

I call over the waiter. "Can I get ice, stat?"

Isa just sits there, her mouth a little open, like she can't quite believe what's happened. "Are you okay?" I ask. "Shit, Isa, I am so sorry. I am so, so sorry."

I reach out to touch her hand, but she draws back very suddenly, like I'm going to hurt her. I sit back in my chair, and the waiter comes over with a little baggie of ice. I wrap it in my cloth napkin and put it in her hand. "Press it to your cheek. Please," I whisper. "It'll make it feel better."

"Should I call the police?" the waiter asks, very quietly. But it's no good. Everyone in the restaurant hears the question.

"Yes," I say, before I realize that the police would find more wrong with the situation than someone hitting Isa.

Much more.

But there's nothing else to do, I guess. Elaine *hurt* her.

"No," Isa says, snapping out of her trance. She glares at me. "No, I don't need the attention." She stands up suddenly and stalks out of the restaurant, holding the ice to her cheek. I follow her outside, and she half runs, half stumbles through the decorative rock gravel in the parking lot.

"Isa," I call after her.

She stops at the passenger side door of my Jeep and spins around. "What?" she snaps. "What do you want to say?"

I hesitate, a few feet away. "I—I'm sorry, Isa. I had no idea she would be there."

"I know *that*," she spits. "Even you wouldn't have taken me somewhere to get physically assaulted."

"Never." I move a step closer. "Let me see your cheek."

She draws the cold pack away and throws it, hard, on the ground. The ice has turned her face an even brighter shade of red, and her eyes are filled with tears. I pick it up and try to rewrap the ice, but bits of dirt cling to the wet plastic bag.

"You didn't think, just maybe, it'd be a good idea to dump that old bitch before you asked me out?" Isa isn't yelling, but she may as well be. Her tone is like a snakebite. Poisonous.

"I wasn't dating her," I say. "I was never dating her."

Of course, that wasn't the way Elaine saw it. But Elaine wasn't into playing fair. She didn't listen to the rules.

"Well, she didn't think that," Isa says. A tear trickles down her cheek. "You might have reminded her."

"But it was never like that!" I say. "It was . . . physical. She got jealous."

Isa raises her voice. "Oh great. I just got slapped by your filthy sex slave? Ugh! Did it occur to you that she's *old*? That this is illegal? That she could go to *jail*? What would her family think of her? And freaking seriously, what would everyone think of you?" She crosses her arms. "Don't you even care about that?"

I shrug. "She was just my mom's friend. It got a little out of hand."

More than a little.

"Ugh," Isa says. "Finn, you—you're messed up. And I can't believe I ever liked you. My first instinct was that you were a sexist asshole. And you know what? I was right." She turns away from me and pulls at the car door. But I haven't unlocked it, and she rests her forehead against the window.

She's crying. Tears are streaming down her cheeks.

"Isa," I say. I touch her arm.

"Get off me, Finn," she whispers. "Just drive me home, okay? I live in the fucking Parlour West Trailer Park. Just drop me off there."

That seems . . . off. Isa, whose parents are successful

musicians, living in the shittiest trailer park in the city? But I don't question it. I nod. "Okay." I unlock the Jeep, and she climbs inside before slamming the door. The trailing part of her purple dress is caught in the door. I open it and push it inside, then walk around to the driver's side.

I start the car, and sit for a moment in the driver's seat. A minute or two passes, and a couple exits the restaurant, pointing at my Jeep. I wish I had tinted windows. I look over at Isa. Her face is swollen. From crying or the slap, I can't tell.

"I'm so sorry, Isa. If I could change everything—I would. I'd do anything to make this right."

She grabs a fast-food napkin I had tucked in a cup holder and dries her eyes. "Finn, can you do me a favor?" she asks. Her voice comes out choked.

"Whatever you want."

She turns in her seat to face me. "Just shut up, okay?" she whispers. "Take me back. And then never, ever talk to me again."

Xavi
Tuesday

I, Xavi Diane Mitchell, belong in jail. Or somewhere where I can get help.

Because I have committed a crime. The worst sort of social taboo. The kind of stuff that would probably get me stoned in olden times.

I kissed my stepbrother.

And the worst, most horrible, most shameful part is: *I liked it.*

"What's wrong, Xavi?" Finn asks. He slides in next to me at the bar. Rico's on the opposite end, pouring a few nightcaps for lingering patrons who look more blitzed than sorority girls on rush night. Or week. Whatever.

"Who said anything was wrong?" I ask. I meant to be all light and carefree and ooh-la-la, but I pitch my voice too high and end up a little more on the singing chipmunk spectrum.

"I've known you for ages," Finn says. "And you don't exactly have the world's best poker face. I always know what you're feeling."

"Fine, Finn." I turn my water glass in circles. "Tell me what I'm feeling, then, since you're such an expert."

Either the sarcasm goes right over his head or he completely ignores it. He leans over the bar and pours himself a Coke. Rico doesn't stop paying attention to the drunk ass dudes at the end of the bar, who are probably going to tip his face off because they stopped being able to tell the difference between Benjamin and Washington, like, two hours ago. Finn could totally be stealing actual liquor and Rico wouldn't even notice.

"You're conflicted," Finn says. "Like, you're not sure how you feel about something, or you did something you're not sure about. And you're—you're a little scared, maybe. I think. And you have a secret. You definitely have a secret." He points at me and clicks his tongue. "How did I do?"

Damn. Finn is pretty good. *Too* good.

"What did Peter tell you?" I ask. That asshole! He's probably out there telling everyone we kissed. It's probably his Facebook status. Oh my damn. Everyone's going to think I'm sleeping with my stepbrother. That's like *incest*. Almost.

"Peter?" Finn looks confused. "What about Peter?"

I put my face in my hands and make a frustrated noise.

Finn nudges me. "What, Xavi? Tell me. Just—get it off your chest. You know I can keep a secret."

And Finn can. When I told him that Carlotta Freeman sabotaged me in last year's home economics sew-off, I know he wanted to tell someone, badly, because Carlotta is generally a horrible person and definitely the type who would use fake handicapped stickers to get good parking spaces. But I asked Finn not to do it, and so he didn't. He's sweet like that.

I check to make sure Rico's still down at the end of the bar, then lean in to Finn's ear.

"I kissed Peter," I whisper.

"Uh. So what?" Finn looks even more puzzled.

"Um, he's my stepbrother, Finn?" I spin my glass on the counter. It slides easily, the condensation beneath the glass making the surface überslippery. "That's gross, right?"

Finn shakes his head and swivels on his barstool so he's facing me. I pretend not to notice and take a sip of my water. "Look at me, Xavi."

I turn toward him. "What."

Finn puts a hand on my wrist. "It's not like he's really your brother. In fact, it's not like he's your brother at all. Your mom has had, like, what? Three other marriages? You probably have eight other brothers out there. If you stop dating people you're sort of kind of related to, then you're going to have to move to Canada and live in an igloo."

I smile a little. Poor, sweet Finn. Canadians in igloos. Sure. But maybe his point's not all bad. If there's one person in this whole stupid restaurant with a good heart, it's Finn.

"Do you like him?" Finn asks, his voice gentle.

"No." I let my hair fall in front of my face. I might be lying, but I'm not sure.

Finn puts his hands on his own legs. "Just think about it, Xavi, okay?" His face turns a little strange. "No one should be judged on who they love. Unless they love Hitler. Then maybe we can judge a little."

Huh. That's kind of a weird thing for Finn to say. I study his face, but for once, he's not giving anything away. "You okay, Finn, buddy?"

"Fine." He drinks down his Coke quickly and slams it on the bar. "Mmm," he says. "Wish this were something stronger." He pumps his arms back and forth. "Let's get another." He leans over the bar, scoops up more ice, and fills his glass again without bothering to wash it. He toasts Rico, who just nods and gives a little wave.

Ugh. Normal Finn is back. "Finn—"

"Gotta get out of here, Xavi. Meeting someone special a little later." His gives me this overdramatic, roguish wink, only he's not very good at winking so both eyes sort of close.

"Right. Go, have fun." I try to keep the disappointment out of my voice.

Finn pauses. "Just don't forget what I said, okay, Mitchell?" He reaches out and musses my hair in an annoying big brother way.

I nod. "I won't."

But it doesn't mean I'll believe him either.

Finn stalks off toward the kitchens, and my phone vibrates. I check the caller ID. *Mom.*

I let it vibrate for a couple of rings. My mom's sort of an insomniac, so it's not really surprising she's calling me this late. She knows I'm still at the restaurant.

I watch it vibrate across the bar, and I snatch it before it falls off the edge. "Hello?"

"Hey, sweetie. How's your night?"

"Fine. You?"

"I'm great. Listen, something wonderful happened today, and I just had to call and tell you. Has your shift slowed down enough that you can talk?"

I glance around the almost-deserted restaurant. "Um, sure, Mom. I can spare a second."

"Good." Her voice is rosy and upbeat. Rare for her, really. "I was at the community center because they're doing these amazing spin classes—weird, right?—anyway,

I spoke to the activities coordinator, and guess what?"

"What?" Does she want to sign us up for mother-and-daughter yoga? My friend Mara did that with her mom and they ended up emulating all of this weird womb crap. Um, count me out.

"Well, you know how you like fashion? And how you're really good at sewing?"

"Sure?" I wait. She's not actually considering design school, is she? Maybe she has a contact. Maybe she met someone who convinced her.

"Well, Dorothy Andersen is hosting a *sewing class*. It's very advanced, and they're sewing their own sixteenth century ball gowns at the end of it as a big final project. It's a few months away, it starts in November, but I know how much you love sewing, so I've signed you up early. How wonderful is that?"

Oh no. Not another sewing class. The last one . . . well, the last one, I could've taught. But she sounds so happy I can't exactly disappoint her. I take my pack of cigarettes out of my pocket and put one in my mouth. Rico shoots me a look, but he knows I won't light it. "It's pretty great, Mom. Thanks." I hope my oh-so-happy works better on her than it did on Finn.

"And get this. Paula Dailey, who owns the Pretty Pocket on First Street? She says you might be able to get a part-time job there next summer if you don't want to be a busgirl anymore!"

Oh no. I'll make half of what I do now. I'll be stuck stocking kitschy fabrics and helping old ladies choose which brass button best matches their coats. And I'll never, ever have a chance at design school. Mom would die before she helped me fund anything out of state. She doesn't want me that far away.

"Um, great, Mom." I hesitate. "But, actually, I have good news. About this summer. And maybe next."

"What is it, honey?" She's genuinely interested. Genuinely happy. My words stick in my throat for a painful half moment.

I glance down the bar, where Rico is clinking shot glasses with his drunk patrons. "I just got promoted to waitress."

"Honey!" Mom squeals. "That's so great! I'm so happy for you! Wait until I tell your stepfather. He's going to be so proud of you! I know how much you wanted this, and you've worked so hard."

No, he isn't. And she won't be proud either. "Thanks, Mom."

"I'm going to go, but when you get home, let's have ice cream to celebrate, okay?" Ice cream is my mom's guilty pleasure. She only eats it, like, twice a year, but she always has a couple of pints of Ben & Jerry's in the basement freezer for emergencies and big celebrations. Apparently, this qualifies.

"Okay."

My mom hangs up, and I watch Rico cash the drunk guys out. Or rather, they throw some bills at him and he waves them out the door, laughing. He notices me staring. "What?" he asks. "Something to say, X?"

I hate that he called me X. But I don't say it, not right away. Instead, I watch him intently for a second more.

"Rico . . . I need a word."

Peter
Wednesday

It's glittery.

It's straight-up nasty.

It should cover a *lot more*.

It's Finn's banana hammock.

And—I can't believe I'm actually going to admit this as a straight dude—he's kind of pwning it.

He struts into the restaurant like a slightly more, uh, gifted, statue of David, a white T-shirt slung over his shoulder and a tiny, weird banana hammock stretched to the limit over his . . . predicament. He grins widely, and his face isn't even red. He's acting even cockier than normal.

And the *mayor* is here. The mayor who requested Finn *personally* to wait her table.

This is not going to fly. Finn could not have picked a worse day to showcase his goods.

Finn walks over to Mayor Field's table.

"Hello, Mayor," he says, very smoothly. He strikes a bodybuilder pose, one arm curled up. "Might I take your order?"

I almost drop the bottle of champagne I'm holding.

Mayor Fields turns fifty shades of red. "Uh, Finn?" she

says, a smile creeping across her face. "I think you may have forgotten your pants today."

Finn drops the posing and looks down, like he only just realized he's basically butt-ass naked. "Oh, right. Does it bother you?"

It bothers *me*. Seeing as how I can mostly just see his ass. How much do you have to work out to get chiseled ass cheeks, anyway? I'd have to check out my ass in the mirror later to be certain, but I'm pretty sure there's nothing chiseled about it.

Xavi walks out, an empty tray balanced below her breast. She stares, her mouth slightly open, and then she laughs.

By now, the whole restaurant has turned to watch Finn in his bright thong. He turns away from the mayor, and she legit *gapes at his ass*.

The Mayor. The one who led the Keep Our Community Wholesome campaign. Is staring at Finn's ass. She almost looks a little . . . excited. Appreciative.

A little less like she has the Bill of Rights stuck up her butt.

It's actually a good look for her.

Finn walks up to the bar. "I think a nice Malbec for the lady," he says. "Something expensive."

He's enjoying this. He's actually *enjoying* this.

"You chose a good day," I mutter. "When the mayor's here."

Finn shrugs. "Better than when kids are here."

Oh. That's what Finn's been waiting for. No kids. He's sort of a good dude even when he's pretending to be a stripper.

I pour the red wine and push it across the bar. "Well," I say. "Enjoy. Don't be offended, but I'm probably going to have a few nightmares." I can't say the same for Jeremiah, who's standing across the room, a look of complete and utter admiration on his face that I'm willing to bet he's never shown to Aida.

Finn steps away, holding the glass sort of delicately. "Should I dance?" he asks, swinging his hips.

"Dear God, for all that is good and holy, please, do not shake that." I hold my hands up, blocking out his . . . circumstantial evidence. Ugh. Seriously. It's true that all guys have a serious love affair with their own junk, but Finn's taking it a little too far.

And so far—even though we're in the finest, most upstanding restaurant in town—no one's complaining.

No one.

What is wrong with people?

Finally some dude in a long black coat gets up, making these choking noises, and stalks toward the door, followed a bit reluctantly by his wife, who keeps casting these long glances back at Finn.

"Come on, Margaret!" barks Black Coat from the doorway.

"I'm calling it, Finn," I say. "Go get dressed."

Finn does one last lap around the floor. One of my middle-aged women at the bar throws a twenty at him, which he gleefully stuffs in his thong.

Finally he disappears into the kitchen, and one of the women sitting at the bar turns to me. "You know," she says, trailing her finger along the rim of her champagne glass, "if you dressed up like that, I might come around here more often."

Now, more than ever, I am thrilled I did not win that dare.

I fake-laugh. "Not likely. Sorry. I'm just here to fill your drinks."

Xavi comes up to the bar, her eyes wide. "Did that just happen?" she asks. "That *just* happened."

"It happened," I agree. "This day is probably going to live in infamy forever. No one can go back to who they were before this horrible, tragic day. A moment of silence, please."

Xavi stands on the bottom metallic circle of a barstool and leans over to give me a buddy punch on the arm. A buddy punch, really? That's what I get after a kiss? "It wasn't so bad, was it?" she asks. "He looks good like that."

I groan. "If you would just man the bar, I need to go stab out my eyes with those little plastic drink swords."

She giggles at me, her hand over her mouth. "I liked it," she says.

And for some reason, even though I know Finn's more of a brother to her than I am, I feel a fiery hot pit of jealousy flame up, deep in my stomach.

Rico walks out onto the floor, probably as damage control, in case there's anyone who's threatening to sue or call in a health inspector or something. What he finds instead is a restaurant full of really happy, shell-shocked people. Even the mayor's still smiling oddly.

I glance over at Xavi, and she's watching Rico, but her whole demeanor has changed. Her shoulders are slumped, her face is a carefully blank slate, but her eyes are pools of unshed tears, which she's trying to hide behind a few strands of hair.

"What's wrong, Xavi?" I ask gently, and she turns her back to Rico.

She shakes her head. "It's nothing, Peter. Just leave me be for a second, okay?"

I want to press her but . . . I don't. I don't want to hurt her worse than someone—probably Rico—already has. What did he do to her? I'll kill him if he hurt her. I will. I reach out to touch her hand, but she jerks away and steps off the barstool. Xavi pushes past Rico, going back into the kitchen without filling her tray. I want to go after her, but she asked me not to. Was that a girl trick, like, saying one thing and meaning another?

Before I can decide, Finn struts back out, fully clothed like he hadn't just paraded around the room in his skivvies.

"Sorry about that, Mayor," he says, grinning widely as he approaches her table. "I've just put your order in."

Finn. A class act.

Rico walks up to the bar, grinning. "Can you get me a scotch?" he asks. He raises his eyebrows at the women, who giggle into their champagne.

I grab the cheapest bottle and give him a sloppy, small pour.

He examines it. A few drops of scotch dribble down the side and land on his white shirt as he takes a sip. "Kind of a small drink, Peter," he says.

"Kind of still morning, Rico." It sounds a little more acid than I intend.

He grins and checks out his expensive watch. "Not for long, though." He gulps down the rest of the scotch. "Not for long." He lowers his voice and leans over the bar. "By the way, seeing as how I'm promoting your little sister to waitress, we're having an extra, celebratory game of Tips this weekend. Are you in?"

"Wouldn't miss it." I could use the cash. And I wouldn't mind keeping an eye on Xavi. Especially since she will likely be entering every time now that she's pulling waitress-level dough.

"My man!" Rico puts out his fist. It almost kills me to return the bump, but I hold out my hand and do a sort of rub/bump, which turns out feeling way more intimate than if I'd just manned up and bumped him.

"Ugh," Rico says. "Okay, dude."

I ignore him and begin wiping down the counter. He did something to Xavi. I know it. And I'm going to find out what.

And then . . . Rico is going down.

Isa
Thursday

For some reason, Rico is holding Tips again.

It hasn't even been two weeks.

And the weirdest part is suddenly everyone's all *Xavi, Xavi, Xavi.* I mean, I get it, she's gorgeous, and yeah, she's kind of funny, and sure, she's nice, but now she gets the best of everything?

Xavi is the type of girl you really want to hate, but she's so cool and sweet that you can't actually feel any sort of ill will toward her without feeling like a cartoon villain.

I walk out onto the floor, balancing my tray on my shoulder. Xavi's working the shift with me—the *busy* shift. New waitresses normally start out on the morning shift, or sneak in a few slow afternoon hours while they're trained. But not Xavi. Rico's put her in prime time: dinner and close.

Even worse, she's good. *Really* good. She is a born waitress. The customers love her, and her pockets are already overflowing with cash. I saw Mr. Phillips, a local dentist, tip her forty dollars on an eighty-dollar meal. I mean, sure, that stuff happens sometimes, but for a brand-new waitress?

It's rare. More than rare.

As I clear my last table, Xavi walks out, grinning like a maniac. "This is great sorts of greatness," she announces to the almost empty room. Peter is cleaning up in the kitchen— he worked a double shift, first at the bar, then as the cook— and Finn, who worked the final shift with us, is nowhere to be found. I think he's avoiding me.

Which I'm fine with. The bruise on my cheek is darker and bigger than I'd thought. I'd had to use pageant levels of makeup to hide it. I don't want him to see how much his ancient girlfriend hurt me.

Or how much he's hurt me.

"You're doing really well," I tell Xavi. "Better than I did, at first." I set a couple of water glasses on my tray.

Xavi actually turns a little pink. "Um, thanks. Rico said you guys were short tonight. I was glad to jump in."

We were short? I frown. I'm pretty sure Aida was bitching yesterday about wanting the late shift, but whatever.

"You know," Xavi says, "I still have a table here. If you feel like ditching a couple minutes early." She jerks her head toward the door as she begins stacking plates onto my tray.

I stare. This is why no one in the whole world can hate Xavi. "Are you sure? I don't mind staying."

Xavi shrugs. "I don't care. It gives me a reason to be on the floor in case my last table decides they need an extra olive on their salads." She grins. "Go on. I got this."

"Thanks, Xavi. I really, really appreciate it. You're the best. Seriously."

"Have fun," she says, bending over my final table.

Huh. People are weird sometimes.

I change back into civilian clothing in the staff bathroom.

I learned my lesson at Finn's boat party—no one stays in their waiting clothes outside of work. In fact, most people don't even *come* to work in their waiting gear. It's best to spend as little time in work clothes as possible.

I emerge a few minutes later, grab my folded clothes and purse, clock out, and head out the back door. Rico will lock up, so I'm not worried.

A light breeze tosses my hair, though it's too little to make any difference. It had to be over a hundred degrees today, and the night has done little to bring the temperature down.

I look toward the water, and at the white light of the moon reflecting off the bay. Maybe I'll roll up these damned jeans—as much as I can, at least, seeing as how they're practically skintight—and sit on the dock outside the restaurant for a minute. I could dangle my toes into the water and watch the sky before I have to retreat to the cloud of cigarette smoke that is the trailer.

I set my clothes and my purse in my rust bucket of a car, shove my keys deep in my pocket, and walk down toward the water. Suddenly, I sort of wish my date with Finn had gone better. It would be nice to hold someone's hand and walk along the shoreline, collect sand in our shoes, and kiss under the clear sky.

But of course, that's stupid. That's silly. Totally cliché.

And with Finn? *Ugh.*

I walk closer to the dock, and I see that someone *is* making quite the opportunity out of necking under the full moon.

I take a couple of small steps closer. Who *is* that? They basically look like they're going to devour each other. I can even hear the moans from here.

I'm actually sort of curious. Is it one of our customers? The lame couple I had to serve tonight who couldn't keep their tongues out of each other's mouths? Or . . . is that someone from the restaurant? My heart beats a little faster.

I step closer, the sand making my footsteps quiet, and realize two things.

First, the couple isn't just necking. The woman's skirt is hiked up and her legs are wrapped around the dude's waist. They're full on *doing it*. On the dock. Where anyone could walk up on them.

Secondly . . .

Holy. Shit.

"Finn?"

It is. Plain as day.

Finn, doing some chick on the dock in broad . . . moonlight.

First, his ancient girlfriend slaps me on our date, and now he's already on to someone else? Literally *onto* someone else?

I'm going to kill him. I am going to *murder* him. I am going to become one of those crazy women in a prison TV show, because Finn is going to die.

"Isa!" Finn pushes himself up, and the woman sits up slightly—Oh shit. Oh holy *shit*.

It's the mayor.

It's the goddamned *mayor*.

I press my hands to my mouth, feeling ill.

"Hold up!" Finn hops up, his jeans loose. I turn away and run, through the sand to the asphalt behind the restaurant. Finn is faster, and he catches me at my car. He grabs me by the arms. His unbuttoned jeans hang loosely around his hips.

"Get off me!" I scream, ripping myself out of his grasp. He holds up his hands, palms out.

"I'm sorry, Isa," he says. "I am so, so sorry. I get what this looks like, okay? I do."

"Like you're a filthy asshole?" I ask. "Yeah, I got that."

He pauses, and his face loosens slightly, like he's relieved. Relieved? But why?

And suddenly, all the little puzzle pieces fall into their perfect places and everything makes sense.

Everything.

Why Finn "dated" Elaine. Why he's sleeping with Mayor Fields. Why all of the richest customers request him.

Why he gets insanely large tips from these "special" customers.

Beautiful, offensive Finn—the quarterback of the football team—isn't just a waiter.

Oh no.

He's a hooker.

He reaches out again. "Isa, Please."

"Get your dirty hands off me!" I screech at him.

He looks at me, stricken. "Don't tell. Please. It would ruin me. And it would ruin Jamie—Mayor Fields, I mean. Please don't tell."

I sneer at him and slam the door to my car. "Next time, Finn, don't be such a slut."

My tires kick up gravel as I speed away.

Finn
Thursday

Isa's car speeds away, kicking stinging little pieces of gravel onto my ankles.

She knows.

Isa Sanchez *knows.*

My heart thuds in my chest like a bass drum, the only instrument Mr. Falferth thought me capable of playing in middle school before he realized I had as much rhythm as a tree stump.

I wonder if they have band in juvie. Or more likely, jail, since I'm seventeen and I'll probably be tried as an adult.

I feel calm and sick all at once, like someone's just explained to me I'm going to die and there's absolutely nothing I can do about it.

"Finn?" Jamie—the mayor—walks up beside me, and stands with me in the back parking lot.

I am quiet for a few seconds, watching the red of Isa's taillights as she rounds the corner toward the main road.

She must be so hurt.

And *I* did that.

I hurt her. Twice. Whatever it is that comes to me, I deserve it.

"She knows," I tell her. "Jamie . . . Isa knows."

The mayor stands next to me silently for a few moments. She reaches down and straightens her skirt. "Will she tell?" she asks, her tone brusque. I imagine this is the voice she uses for campaigns. To run meetings. To tell her assistant to get her coffee.

I don't meet Jamie's eyes. "She might." I turn away from the parking lot—the last thing I need right now is for Xavi to see me down here with the mayor—and head back to the dock where my belt and wallet sit, tossed somewhere near the mayor's high heels and purse.

Mayor Fields follows.

"What do you mean, 'she might'?" the mayor asks. Her tone is surprisingly calm. I get the feeling she's sort of like an iceberg person: She shows only a little of what she's feeling on the surface, but she's got a lot more going on underneath.

"I mean she's pissed at me." I grab my belt off the dock and begin threading it through my jeans. My hands shake slightly. "I asked her out last week and completely embarrassed her because one of my overly attached clients slapped her in the face while we were at dinner. Hard. In front of a bunch of people."

The mayor's face is pale in the moonlight. "And now she wants revenge."

"Maybe." I tuck my wallet back into my pocket.

"Finn," the mayor says. "If I'm caught, I lose my job. I'll probably go to prison. And so will a lot of other really good people who use you."

What a weird thing to say. A lot of really good people who

use me. I shake my head, trying to get my thoughts into some sort of sense. "I know."

The mayor looks up at me, and her eyes are different. They're hard. She takes my hands in hers, but there's no real comfort in the action. "She can't tell. You have to convince her."

"I don't know if I can, Jamie," I say. I pull away and slam my hand down on a wooden post. "She hates me. She hates me so much." I look out at the water. An hour ago, it all looked so calm. So peaceful. What a crock of shit.

She moves behind me, and her hands find my shoulders. "Finn, I'm going to tell you what to do, okay? And you're going to listen. I'm good at addressing these . . . problematic situations."

I laugh, but my chest feels weird and empty, devoid of fear or pain or anything. It's all gone. It's over. I can't see how this can be fixed.

"Well, first and foremost, you're going to stay very calm. Rico is a good friend of mine. I don't want him knowing anything is going on. He's not a good man."

I raise my eyebrows.

"What?" Jamie asks. She buttons her suit jacket very precisely. "You think I don't know about his stupid rooftops games? And his tax evasion? And the other things he does to keep his twisted little empire running?"

"Okay." I don't really care about Rico. I won't tell him.

"And you," she says, "need to quit."

"Waiting?" I ask. "I can't."

She shoots me a look. She gets impatient with me sometimes. "No, Finn. Your little side venture here. I'm not even saying that because we got caught. I'm saying that because as long as you do this thing, as long as you have this little business, you'll never have anyone in your life. Do you understand?"

I nod. She means Isa and I would have had a nice dinner. Or maybe it would have sucked. But at least it wouldn't have been interrupted by Elaine slapping the ever-loving shit out of her. And she's right. This isn't good for me. It's not just that it's dangerous. It's so wrong. My parents would hate me if they knew. My brothers, too.

"And third," she says, "I know you've been saving this money because you're concerned you'll never get into college. Am I incorrect?"

I shake my head. There's a reason why she's mayor. She's smart.

"Don't you think a long, glowing, personalized recommendation from the mayor would get you into a school, even if you have a little trouble with your grades now and again?"

I stand up a little straighter. "Yes, ma'am."

She glowers at me. "Don't call me ma'am. It makes me feel ancient."

"Okay. So you're going to write me a letter?"

Jamie nods. "I'll write you the best recommendation you'll ever get. One caveat, however: You need to find Isa. And you need to make sure she never, ever tells."

"How?" I ask. "Isa's a good girl. I can't just *bribe* her."

She narrows her eyes and touches my back, like she's telling me a secret. "Finn, darling. I think you'll be surprised to find nearly everyone has a price tag on them. You just have to figure out whether you're willing to pay it. And with your—ah—talent—I think you'll figure something out."

"Right." Her comment stings. I don't think she means it as a compliment.

She smiles at me and pats my hand. "If you do that, my boy, everything you've been working for will be within your grasp."

Yes.

Everything.

Sure.

Xavi
Saturday
2:26 a.m.

I sit at my sewing machine, a long roll of expensive fabric over my lap. I haven't made one stupid stitch on this extraordinary pattern. And I didn't even work today.

I could have, but I didn't. I didn't want the extra shift. The extra cash. The patrons who are requesting *me*, now.

And the reason why.

I am Floozy McFloozypants from Floozerville by way of Skankland. I have a PhD in Slore.

But that doesn't mean I'll miss Tips tonight. I can't miss that. I won't. But I can't be there, at the restaurant, all day. I need time at home. Time to hide.

I put my head in my hands and shut my eyes.

All I can think about is those slightly blurry Polaroids. I haven't even had *sex* and I'm the girl who sent naked photos to her boss. I was careful, though. I cropped the top half of my face out of all of them. And they are all a little blurry, like cell phone pictures from your drunk BFF.

But not blurry enough.

And I still gave them to Rico. I passed them to him in an unmarked envelope.

I stare down at the fabric.

"Was it worth it?" I ask out loud.

It's going to be. It has to be. I glance at the clock and stand up from my sewing machine. It's almost time for Tips. And seeing as I have eternal free entries, I'm not going to miss it. Even if that means facing Rico.

I shudder.

I walk into the restaurant about twenty minutes later. It isn't that far from my house, but I sat alone in my car for a few minutes, staring at the clock on my dashboard as the minutes ticked by.

Then, eventually, I opened my door and climbed up to the roof, where everyone's already waiting.

"Xavi!" Jake shouts, pumping his hands in the air. "Shots!" He tosses me a little plastic shot glass—the prepackaged kind you have to shake and take.

It's exactly what I need. I peel the little aluminum foil circle from the top and down the drink. It tastes exactly like it should—plastic-y, old, and too strong. Like something from the clearance aisle in the liquor store. A nice shot for self-hatred.

I toss the glass into a dented metal trash bucket someone's dragged up. It makes a loud metallic sound.

"Just in time," Rico says. "Aida's about to reveal the dare." He cocks his finger at her and looks in her direction.

Aida smiles tightly without showing any teeth. Her arms are crossed over her chest. Uh-oh. If I were going to skip out on anyone's dares, it'd be Aida's. She's super demonic. Everyone else's challenges have a hint of fun, but Aida goes straight to danger. Like, you-might-die-from-this danger. Last summer, she made Finn walk a slack line strung from a tall tree in the parking lot to the top of the roof. Fortunately, Finn is a badass, and when he fell he caught the line with both hands and dropped down onto an SUV without turning into a bloody sidewalk smear. But if it were Jake on that slack line? He has zero athletic ability and would have totally eaten it, face-first in the concrete.

I join the circle of players around the bonfire. Everyone's in tonight. Everyone but Finn. In fact, Finn isn't anywhere to be found. Something's not right. Tips isn't Tips without him here. He'd never, ever miss a game. He'd never, ever turn down a dare.

Something's wrong. I nudge Isa, who is standing next to me. "Where's Finn?" I whisper. Isa should know if anyone does. I heard that Finn asked Isa out, and Isa actually said yes. Total first. Total shocker move for Finn, too. He isn't into high school girls. Or girls at all, some people say.

She looks straight ahead, but her face turns cold and hard. "I don't know and I don't care."

Well. Guess the date didn't go all that well.

Aida shoots us both *shut-up* looks and clasps her hands together in front of her chest. "The dare," she says, "is one hookup between two restaurant employees. This must happen during the hours when we are open, when patrons are in the restaurant. The hookup must happen out on the floor, not in the kitchen or bathroom. Evidence of the hookup must be provided. And if you are caught by any customers, you forgo the pot."

I look around the circle. Peter stares at me, but I ignore the feeling his eyes give me. It's like he knows something is wrong.

No one sits. Warren fidgets, but stays standing. And then, suddenly, Josh thumps back into his chair, his arms folded over his chest, followed by Celia. I don't know why Celia keeps buying in. She never goes in for any of the dares, anyway. Jeremiah winks at Aida. This is an easy dare for him. All he has to do is hook up with his girlfriend in secret.

Do I want to do this? What does hooking up mean? It can't mean sex. If it meant sex, I wouldn't do it. I'd sit down.

But then, maybe I wouldn't. I think of the pictures, and my stomach feels strange, like something is alive inside of it, writhing around. It's Aida's own fault if she doesn't clarify the dare further. Hooking up could totally just be kissing.

I lock my knees. I'm so not sitting.

"All right. The hat, please, Rico?" Aida asks.

"Of course." He grins at me and pulls a hat out of the pocket of his jeans. "I want Jake to pick. Names in, everyone."

I pull a crumpled bill from my pocket. I steal a Bic pen from Isa and scribble an X on it before dropping it in the hat.

Aida frowns, her thick eyebrows drawing together. "Um, sure." She walks over to Jake and holds the hat as high as she can, which still isn't high enough for tall, gangly Jake. He pulls out a folding chair and she steps up on top of it. Jake reaches up into the hat, fumbles for a bill, and pulls a very crumpled one out.

A very familiar-looking wrinkled-up bill.

He smoothes it out over his knee, taking his time. Then he holds it up above his head, one hand on either side, like it's a trophy belt.

"Xavi," he says, showing everyone my Abraham Lincoln.

Across the circle, Peter starts, like he's been jolted.

I take a deep breath, and Rico collects the bills and shoves them into his pocket. "So who's it going to be, Xavi?" he asks, grinning at me. "I think you have the pick of the litter."

Um, ew much?

"I don't have to choose now." I toss my bill at Rico, and it lands at his feet. "You'll all know when or if you need to."

His creepster grin falters for a half second, but then is back in place, bigger and smarmier than before.

And I realize I'm done. Just . . . done. I don't want to be around these people right now. I don't want to be around Rico. I'm going to wander around until I lose the small buzz that one cheap shot has given me and then I'm going to drive home. Maybe I'll drive out into the pasture, to the little tumbledown shed, and spend what's left of the night with the stars.

More beers are passed around. Celia hands one to me, but I put it quietly back in the cooler to swim in the half-melted ice and grab a water instead. I tuck it into my shirt and climb downstairs.

No one stops me.

No one notices.

I sit down at a table in the dark restaurant. The only light comes from a glowing red exit sign above the door. The only noise is the music from above and the faint buzzing from the red light.

I uncap my water and take a long drink. I want to get out of here, and the faster I down it, the faster I get to leave and be alone again. Why did I take that shot? Did I think I was going to be able to morph back into Fun Party Girl and totally brush off my shame?

Yep.

I had thought that.

Talk about being wrong.

I see the shape emerge from the kitchen before I can tell who it is. I stay still and quiet; the person's eyes won't have adjusted enough from the florescent light of the kitchens to tell I'm here.

"Xavi?" the shape calls quietly. "You down here?"

It's Peter.

I swallow hard, trying to distinguish the feelings floating around in my chest.

Peter's the one I want to be with. He's the only one I want to kiss. He makes me feel good and safe and better.

But the feeling is wrong, so I don't answer. I watch him walk out the door to search for me in the parking lot, and I quietly slip out the back.

Peter

Monday

I'm pouring a stiff scotch for an older gentleman who is legitimately wearing tails when I see her.

Xavi.

White faced and pale.

Her hair is mussed and her gorgeous eyes are empty. Blank. She sees me watching and tries to smile, but it doesn't quite work.

It's three in the afternoon, so neither the bar nor the restaurant is remotely busy, and Rico only has Xavi, Josh, Finn, and me working this shift. Even Rico's not here, and I'm not totally sure he has a life beyond his restaurant. Jake will get here in, like, an hour to start the dishwashing. And Finn is being really weird. He's hardly talked to me or anyone else for that matter. I asked him what was up, and he just shrugged and grunted, so I let him be. Probably has to do with Isa.

But Xavi—Xavi's another issue entirely. I've seen her upset, angry, whatever—but nothing like this. There's a cold determination in her that's as unfamiliar and surprising as her kiss.

I motion her over. She looks back at the kitchen, and then

at me, like she's thinking she might escape, but then she walks over slowly. I meet her at the portion of the bar that curves toward the kitchen, away from the customers.

"Sit," I tell Xavi.

She looks left and right, and climbs onto a barstool. "Can I have a drink?" she asks in a cool tone.

I nod. Xavi isn't very good at holding her alcohol, so I just pour her an orange juice. Finn stalks out of the kitchen without a word and grabs the scotch I've left at the opposite end of the bar.

I'm sort of thankful he doesn't stop to talk.

"What's wrong?" I ask, both hands on the bar.

She sort of smiles again. "Who said anything was wrong?"

I study her carefully arranged expression. "I can tell, Xavi." I lean forward and smooth down her hair, so at odds with everything else about her.

"Of course you can." Her mouth quirks a little again into the semblance of a smile. I can't tell if she's being sarcastic or not.

"Did Rico do something?" I ask. For a moment, her painstakingly crafted mask slips, and her lips thin and her eyes narrow. Then it's gone.

"Everything's fine," she says evenly. She sips her drink and wrinkles her nose. "Juice? Really?"

"Come back here," I say, lifting the panel of the bar that will let her in. "Show me how to mix your favorite drink. I'll mix you one with actual liquor later."

She tilts her head at me in that way she does and slides into the bar. "Might as well. I don't have any tables right now. Everyone wants Finn today, anyway."

I laugh. "Everyone always wants Finn. Don't take it too hard."

She grins a little evilly at me. "Of course not."

I study her. A moment ago, I could have sworn that something was wrong. Really, seriously wrong. But now she's behind the bar, frowning at bottles. As she bends over for a larger glass, a line of flesh appears at her back where her shirt pulls up.

I stare. I can't help it.

"What?" Xavi straightens up. She untangles her mussed hair from its tie and lets it fall down her back. It's creased from being wound so tightly.

"Are you sure you're okay?" I ask.

She helps herself to the Sprite, adds a splash of grenadine and a little lime, and finishes with about six cherries. She takes a sip. "Mmmm," she says, ignoring my question. She comes a little closer and presses the glass to my lips. "Here. Try." She tilts the glass up, and I taste her drink. It's extraordinarily sweet, but—actually not that bad. It's definitely an umbrella drink. It might even be good with a splash of vodka.

"You might make bartender yourself some day," I say, grinning at her. She smiles from behind the glass and downs the rest quickly.

God, I want her. She's close enough to kiss again. And the way she's looking up at me . . .

"Something to say, Peter?"

I blush slightly, and watch her eyes, seeing the way brown flecks decorate the bright green. "You're really beautiful, Xavi."

"You can't say that to me." But she takes another small

step closer. Her hand brushes my chest. "It's very bad. You're my brother."

"Not by blood," I whisper. Her breasts brush against me, but I don't reach for her. No matter how much I want to.

"Not by blood," she repeats.

"It's wrong," I say, but I don't mean it. I don't mean it at all. I just don't want her doing anything she'll regret.

But . . . I need her.

I take a step back. Then another.

She moves forward. . . .

She licks her lips. . . .

And then . . .

She wraps her hand around the back of my neck and pulls my face down to kiss me. Damn, her lips are soft. I wrap my arms around her and pull her closer, and she pulls away, looking wickedly to her left and right.

There's no one around.

"Ever hooked up in the restaurant, Peter?" she asks, and pulls me to the floor.

I stare at her, on the floor beneath me, her hair spread out around her, messy and cute and alluring.

Yes, I have hooked up in the restaurant. A couple of times. But never like this. Never when it meant anything.

Never with anyone I loved.

But I'm not going to tell her that. I kiss her harder, cradling her head away from the hard floor, and she pulls me tight against her body, so I can feel every inch of her through her clothes.

She flicks her tongue against my lips, and she's kissing me harder now, like she wants me as badly as I want her. But that can't be. She hates me. I pull away from her, and watch her for a moment—the way the color is rising in her full cheeks, and her long eyelashes, and the sweet smile on her mouth.

"Are you sure, Xavi?" I ask.

She nods. "Yes. I'm sure."

"And this isn't because of the game?"

She pauses, considering, and her eyes flick away from me for a moment. "No," she says. "This is because of me. And because of you. And because I want you."

I hear Finn's footsteps as he walks by, but I don't care.

"I want you, too," I whisper.

Her fingers find the buttons to my shirt.

Isa
Tuesday

"I need to talk to you."

I look up from the server's booth, where I'm wrapping silverware for tomorrow's diners.

Finn. Of course it is. I ignore him and count out more forks. I'm four short.

"Isa—"

"Go get me another tray of silverware, Finn."

He looks at me for a second longer. "Yeah. Sure." He stalks away, his shoulders slightly hunched over and his powerful, football player hands wrapped into fists. I've pissed him off.

I don't care. After what he did to me, I couldn't give a *shit*.

I've never hated anyone like I've hated Finn. I want to tell him that, but here, in the restaurant, with your Upper-Middle-Class American Family dining two tables over, I can't call him all the horrible names I want to.

I haven't told anyone yet. That the boy I like is actually both the conference quarterback of the year and a sex worker. Part of me wants to tell. Expose him for what he is. Part of me wants to climb up on the table and announce it to everyone. To embarrass the asshole like he embarrassed me with his old girlfriend in that stupid, beautiful restaurant.

But another part of me rather likes having the secret for myself. Something to hold over him. To make him scared. To use him.

And I have a plan.

I should never have liked him. Should never have taken my eye off what I was doing. What I wanted this whole time.

I stack the rolled silverware into a large plastic tub, and Finn comes back dutifully with another tray. He might hate me now, but I have him under my proverbial thumb. I can do whatever I want with him.

And, if all goes according to plan, he'll help me get everything I need.

I smile. Finn's forced pleasant expression drops off his face and lands somewhere at his feet.

"What?" he asks.

"You wanted to talk? Let's talk."

He looks around, like maybe I've somehow booby-trapped the table. "Sit down," I command and he obeys. "Now, tell me what it is you wanted to say." I keep my voice carefully low. We can't let the customers know what we're discussing, after all.

Finn grabs a few napkins and begins rolling the silverware beside me. He takes a deep breath. "First, I just wanted to say I'm sorry. I'm sorry that I ever asked you out while still being . . . involved with my other thing. And I'm sorry about Elaine. She's crazy, and I won't be seeing her anymore. I'm sorry about what you saw. You must think I really suck."

"Oh. I do." I spit the words.

He dutifully rolls another set of silverware. "I get that. But I wanted you to know—I'm quitting. It was wrong, and stupid, and I'm sorry. So I'm done. Forever. And I needed to ask you a favor."

"A favor? From me? Sure, Finn, anything for you. I owe you *so much*."

Either he doesn't catch the sarcasm, or he ignores it. "Uh," he says, "I need you to keep my—secret. Please. It'll ruin a lot of lives if this gets out. And these people—my . . . ah . . . clients—they're not all bad people. Some of them are really nice. And I'm done, anyway. I swear on the Bible. And I go to church every Sunday, Isa. I'm done."

I laugh, and my chest feels cold and hard. "No, Finn. You aren't done."

He blinks stupidly. "What?"

"You're just getting started. Only now that I'm in charge, you're not going to be so careless. Doing the mayor on the dock? Where anyone could have found you? Come on. How idiotic can you be?"

Finn's head jerks up, and a spoon clatters to the floor. He doesn't bend over to pick it up. "What?" he asks, and for a moment, pain flashes across his face. A sharp flash somewhere in my chest reflects his expression, but I ignore it.

I reach my heel over and kick the spoon under the table. "My commission is 40 percent, which I think is more than generous, considering the circumstances. All you have to do is play your horrible little game for the rest of the season, skim me a few of your earnings off the top, and no one will ever learn your dirty little secret." I pause and point at him with a butter knife. "Do we have a deal, Finn?"

Finn doesn't look at me. Very carefully, he finishes wrapping a set of silverware and places it in the Tupperware container with the rest.

"You know," he says, his voice low. "I'm really, really glad we didn't work out."

Finn
Wednesday

I set two plates of duck confit down on the small table.
"Anything else?" I ask.

Mrs. Seiker winks at me and casts an eye toward the
restroom, where her husband has disappeared. "You'll see
when you get the check, darling." She speaks like a hero-
ine from a black-and-white movie. Very proper and full of
importance.

"Sure," I say. "Please keep in mind I'm changing my rates.
It's a 50 percent increase."

Take that, Isa. She said I couldn't quit my business, but
she never said I couldn't up my rates. That's *got* to take out a
good portion of my clientele. And if I don't make as much, Isa
doesn't either. Maybe she'll lose interest.

"Fifty percent!" Mrs. Seiker exclaims, putting her hand on
her chest. "My, my. Aren't we in demand?"

I shift uncomfortably. "Something like that. And remember, cash, or you forgo your . . . service."

"Well," she says, fanning herself a little with her hand.
"I can't say you aren't worth it, darling. Oh, look, here's
Arnold now."

Damn it. So much for losing clientele.

Her husband—a painfully skinny gray-haired man who looks kind of like the grim reaper—sits down opposite her. She grins at me. "Looks great, Finn. Thanks so much."

"If there's nothing else I can get you . . . ," I say, deliberately trailing off. It's a trick of the trade: sound like you're leaving, and they're less likely to ask for more, but they still think you're doing an awesome job.

Arnold Seiker shakes his head. "No, we're good, but watch us closely. I'll be needing another Guinness sooner rather than later."

"Certainly." I incline my head at him and set off toward the kitchen to take a breather. I wish I smoked, or that I had another reason to go outside for a few minutes. Screw it. Rico knows where to find me if someone needs anything. I push out the back door to the staff patio.

Xavi's already outside, playing with her unlit cigarette. I push myself up to sit on the railing next to her. She grins when she sees me. "Finn! I didn't know you were working today!" She gives me a big hug around the middle, the only part of me she can reach while standing on the deck and, strangely, I feel a little better.

"Yeah," I say. "I was bored and Jeremiah called in sick."

"You mean hung over?" she asks, grinning. "If Jeremiah actually has the flu, he caught it from the Jaeger shots he was downing last night at Gerard's." Gerard's is a bar a couple of blocks down, set a little back from the water. It's a great little dive.

"You were there?" I mean, Xavi looks older than sixteen, but she couldn't pass for twenty-one if she tried.

She shakes her head. "Facebook. One shot per photo. He did, like, eight. In the last one, he was stripped down to this stained beater and plaid boxers. Classy stuff." She smiles into the horizon, where the sun would be if it were out today. "He had his arm around this pretty redhead, too."

"So Aida's out?" I ask. It's good to talk to Xavi. She makes me forget.

"Who knows?"

The back door opens with a squeak, and Rico steps outside. Xavi shrinks back, like she's hiding herself behind me, but Rico basically ignores her. "Finn!" he says. "My man!" He holds out his hand, and I slide off the railing so we can do a weird version of a man hug, where he hits my back after. I try not to frown. What's up with him being so friendly?

He wants something. There's no other explanation.

He nods at Xavi. "Whaddup, Triple X?"

Xavi gives him a look that could freeze vodka. "My name is not Triple X, Rico." She grabs onto my arm, like she's using me as some sort of shield.

"Whatever. Listen, Finn, man. We missed you at Tips! My girl Xavi won. First time for everything, right?"

"I heard," I say. "And she completed her dare a couple days ago. I was here. Witness." I point at myself.

"Yeah, Xavi? Who was the lucky man?" Rico leers at Xavi. It looks like he's on the verge of drooling.

"You're a weird dude, Rico," I say. "And Xavi swore me to secrecy." I wink at her.

Xavi nods, her face tight and drawn. "All I had to do was have proof. That was Finn."

Rico chuckles. "You're quite a player, Xavi. And I can always check the cameras."

There are some cameras on the floor, but they're pointing at the door. Everyone knows that. Xavi gets her game face on. "Check them. I don't care. I won, fair and square."

"Then you'll have your money," Rico says. "Finn, you in for this weekend? We're going again. Tips is getting real." He lifts up his hand for a high five.

I ignore his outstretched hand. "Uh. No. I won't be there."

Rico's face turns faintly red. He drops his hand slowly. "Why? You're the man, Finn. You've won more games that anyone else, ever. You're a legend."

"You know Michael Jordan?" I ask. "He was this old basketball player. And he was the man. He won everything. And he retired while he was still awesome."

"You're comparing yourself to Michael Jordan?" Rico smirks. "Really? Who next? Barack Obama?"

I ignore his cut. "Michael Jordan came back." I stop. "That was a mistake. He wasn't at the top of his game anymore. So I guess what I'm saying is—"

"You're done." Rico cuts me off. "You're not playing anymore."

Finn shrugs. "For now, at least. And I guess I probably won't come back."

"Then maybe you don't need to work here anymore," Rico says. "This job is for players only. Or maybe you can go valet out front. I'm sure you'd be good at that. I could get rid of Raj."

"Whatever you think, man." I turn my back to him.

I can feel Rico staring at me for a minute longer, and then he turns away. I hear the door close.

"Oh my damn! That was cold, dude," Xavi says, punching me playfully in the arm.

"Yeah. Rico's a bit of a douche, though."

"Aren't you afraid of actually getting fired?" Xavi puts out her fake cigarette on the railing. "Of him just coming unglued if you're really shitty to him? Getting rid of you?"

I rest my elbows on the railing. "I think everyone knows I don't really need the job. And I think Rico knows that without me he's going to lose an awful lot of people. People that would follow me to, say, General Steakhouse?"

Xavi's sucks her lips in. "You wouldn't," she says. "You're a Watersider."

I straighten up. "You're right."

She touches my arm. "You're not yourself right now, are you?"

"Nope." I look down at her, and her eyes are actually a little glassy.

"What's wrong?"

I shake my head. "You'd hate me if I told you."

"I wouldn't hate you, Finn. You're more of a brother to me than Peter. I could *never* hate you."

"No." I step away from her. I look at her mangled cigarette lying on the wood of the railing, but I don't say anything.

We stand together quietly for a little while.

"Do you know who . . . did you really see me hooking up with someone?" Xavi asks, forcing the words out.

I didn't exactly see it, but I have a pretty good idea. She confessed to me that she kissed Peter, after all. I can't imagine it would be someone else. Not unless she were trying to get Peter out of her head or something.

I nod. "Well, I could hear you. Who were you with?"

She ducks her head and laughs softly. "Can I tell you a secret, Finn? Something you can't tell anyone?"

I nod. I'd do anything for Xavi. A single tear slides out of the corner of her eye and drips down her cheek. Her lip quivers.

"I'm not myself either."

Xavi
Thursday

I sit in the corner of my room, my elbows on my knees and a piece of thread between my fingers. I press it into my thumbs and watch it make thin purple indentations in my skin.

For the first time in my life, I have *money*. Real money. Money that could make a real difference. More cash than will fit in my wallet.

I even totally threw it on my bed and rolled around in it. Then I felt really gross because I know where some of that money has been, so I took a shower and put my comforter in the washer.

Yep, I have cash. And another first for me: I am completely and totally ashamed of myself. Not in the way that your mom says you should be when you're five and you steal something from the cookie jar, but in the real, awful way, that sits in the bottom of your stomach and rots.

Yes, because of the pictures. Yes, because I took them for all of the wrong reasons. Not that I'm saying there are *right* reasons to take pictures like that.

And, yes, because of Peter.

Because I think . . . well . . .

I think I'm in love with him.

And I can't believe I let it get that far. I can't believe I let him do *that*. *Sex*. I always thought my first time would be special. With someone I really cared about. Someone I loved. Probably someone that I was married to, like my mom always said was right.

Someone who wasn't my stepbrother.

I wrap my thread around my finger and watch it turn blue.

But I might love him. I might.

I feel sick.

Something's wrong with me.

There's a knock at my door, and I huddle further into my corner, pressing my back into the wall. I unwind the thread from my finger and the digit pulses like it has a heart.

The knock comes again, twice.

"Xavi?"

Holy shit. It's Peter.

Peter.

My door isn't locked. He could just come in here. And what would he want? To do it again? I can't do it again. I hide my head in my arms and peak out through a spot just under my elbow. I'm not ready. Or I wasn't ready. Or something.

The doorknob turns. Slowly.

"Go away!" I shout.

He peers in. "Xavi—"

I don't lift my head. "Just leave me alone, okay, Peter?"

"I just wanted to tell you Celia's been waiting outside in her car for about twenty minutes. Didn't you mention you were going to catch a movie with her?"

Oh.

Um.

Yeah. Yeah I was. She asked me during the last shift. And I like Celia. She's probably the most decent person at the whole restaurant. Except for Finn, of course.

And, shit, she's probably texted me fifty times, but I've been ignoring my phone.

I lift my head slightly. "I'll be right there."

"Okay." He gives me this weird half smile and closes the door.

I stand up and toss the piece of thread onto my desk. I'm basically the messiest mess of messes right now. But it's the movies. It's dark. And the only guy I like just caught me huddled in a corner like a huge psychopath.

I grab my purse and a light jacket. Celia's sitting outside in her ancient bright-blue Datsun, which has one headlight out and a serious exhaust problem. If anyone can't afford to buy into Tips, it's her—but still, she finds a way, almost every time.

"Hey, girl!" she says cheerfully. Her hair is frizzed out in this beautiful, accidental way that only redheads can pull off. For some reason, Celia is devoted to our cook, Josh, but every guy in the entire world likes her. She's sweet and kind and curvy in the way that fashion magazines look down on but everyone else seems to like.

She drives like a maniac, so we arrive at the theater in about four seconds. Celia is obsessed with slasher flicks, which I sort of don't mind, and they're showing a three-show series for five bucks. Of course, all of the movies came out a million years ago, and you can buy them for practically nothing now, but Celia likes them, so whatever. She pays for the tickets, and I buy one giant tub of popcorn to share and two packs of Sour Patch Kids each. Celia adds two large Diet Cokes to the order.

"Let's sit in the front," I say. "I never get to sit in the front."

And so we do. There's maybe two other people in the entire theater, so we could take up eight rows if we needed to.

"Did you know," Celia says, sneaking a hand into the tub of popcorn, "that this is the only theater in fifty miles that still shows movies on film? Isn't that so cool? Everything else is digital now. It's, like, throwback."

I frown. "Hasn't everything been digital for a thousand years? Is this a theater from the stone ages? We're only missing rocks for seats and torches for electricity."

Celia throws a piece of popcorn at me, giggling. "Shut up. You clearly do not have an appreciation for history."

"And you clearly don't appreciate progress," I say. "Do you still use a landline at home? Oh my damn, I bet you totally do. And I bet you listen to a CD player, like my stepdad, and you attach it to your hip when you go running."

She giggles. "Have you seen my car? I definitely prefer vintage. I totally have a *record* player. And a lava lamp."

"You're like my grandma!" I exclaim, and someone a couple of rows back shushes us. I look up—the screen is very politely asking us to PLEASE TURN OFF YOUR CELL PHONES. I switch mine to silent, like everyone else does.

The credits start with a massive gush of blood, like, the Old Faithful of blood geysers. Celia giggles a little nervously. "This is going to be so scary!" she says as a scythe spins across the screen, ninja style.

And, right then, there is a sharp snap from the bright little window at the back of the theater, and the movie stops before it really starts.

Just like that.

Celia's precious vintage film is broken.

"No!" she groans, throwing a Sour Patch Kid at the screen. She misses entirely and it ends up in the dark abyss beyond the front row.

The guy who shushed us stands up. "It'll be back up in a few minutes," he announces. "This stuff happens all the time with film. All. The. Time."

I settle back in my seat, sighing heavily.

And suddenly, in the lonely blackness of the broken theater, it hits me. All at once. Everything in the last few days just settles on my chest. I blink my eyes rapidly. I will not cry. I will not. But something in my throat grows bigger and heavier. I swallow hard. What am I doing? Crying at the beginning of a slasher flick? Something's wrong with me.

"Hey," Celia says, nudging me. "You okay?"

Damn. I was hoping she wasn't paying any attention to me. I try to smile. "Sure I am."

"You look . . . weird."

I laugh. "Uh, thanks a lot, Cel. Not the look I was going for."

She pops a Sour Patch Kid into her mouth. "No, I mean, it's like something's bothering you. Is something bothering you?"

I drum my fingers on my knee. "Can I, um, tell you something? Something really stupid?"

Celia puts a hand to her chest. "I," she says, "am nothing if not an expert on stupidity. Shoot."

I draw my knees up so my heels are balanced on the edge

of the theater seat. "I think I'm in love with someone."

Celia squeals and clasps her hands. "Ohmygosh, Xavi! That's wonderful! Who is it?"

I take a deep breath. "I can't tell you."

Celia frowns. "Uh, why not? It's not an old dude, right? I will totally freak if it's an old dude. Unless he's super hot. Then it's all good."

"Um. No. It's not. I mean, it's just . . . have you ever been in love with someone who is really, really wrong for you? Like, someone who society would totally go all Romeo and Juliet over? Only worse? Like everyone would hate me because it's so wrong?"

Celia turns in her seat, propping one bent knee up. A few of her candies fall out of the package and onto the sticky theater floor. "Listen," she says, popping up an index finger. "I could give a shit what people say. Love is never wrong. And if you find it, you're lucky. Don't be an idiot and ignore it. If you find it, screw what everyone else thinks. Be with whoever you want to be with and forget it."

The screen flickers back to life.

"Forget everyone else," I repeat.

"Damn straight," Celia affirms.

I wonder if she'd still say that if she knew the truth.

Peter
Sunday

"Peter. Dude. Have you seen Xavi?" Finn drums his fingers on the counter at me.

I pause from testing the broth. "Um. No. I haven't really seen her around much. I think she's supposed to be in for the late shift or something, though." Of course, I'd see her if I could, but I think after the whole sex thing, Xavi's playing the avoidance game. As lame as it is to admit, it's killing me. I sent her an IM last night and she immediately went offline. I knocked on her door and she hid in the corner.

She hates me.

Finn presses his palms on the countertop and stretches his shoulders. "I hung with her yesterday. I wanted to let her know *I* convinced Rico to give her the cash since she hooked up in the restaurant. Girl doesn't waste any time, right?" Finn straightens, then grabs a soda out of the fridge. "Do you mind?"

I freeze on my way to the cutting board. "Hold up, dude. You . . . saw her hook up?" Shit.

"Nah. Heard her. You can't mistake her, ah, sounds." Finn actually looks sort of bashful, but he's right. Xavi has this throaty, gorgeous voice that you could pick out anywhere.

"That's awkward. Do you know who was with her?"

"Dunno. Wasn't me, though. But if Rico was going to question her closely, I'd lie and say it was." He takes a loud swallow of his drink.

"Lying about Tips will get you fired, Finn."

Finn shrugs. "I couldn't give a shit if I get fired. I'm sick as hell of Rico and Isa and everyone else around here."

What the hell? What's with the Finn-shaped evil robot? Finn's *never* like this. But something tells me he's serious. Something's different. On a fundamental level. Something, or someone, has jacked up Finn's compass so it's not pointing north anymore.

And Isa? I thought he'd actually sort of gotten on her good side. Maybe not, though. Finn doesn't exactly have a way with words. It wouldn't be the most unlikely thing in the world if he pissed her off again.

"What happened to you, dude?" I ask. "You seem, I don't know, a little screwed up."

Finn just looks at me. Then he looks away.

And he laughs.

He laughs like I've never heard him laugh, until he bends over with one hand on his stomach and the other hand braced on the counter. When he finally straightens up, he looks at me, dead in the eyes.

"You know how people say that you're never sorry until you get caught?" He still has a strange smile on his mouth, but it doesn't reach anywhere else.

"Yeah. I guess." I still haven't opened the fridge. The mushrooms are sitting in a big silver bowl, waiting to be cut, and customers will be arriving soon.

"I was sorry the whole goddamned time."

I close the fridge and grab onto his shoulder. "Finn. What in the ever-loving hell are you talking about?"

Finn doesn't move. "Nothing, man. Nothing. You wouldn't get it. You don't do shit wrong."

And I laugh too. "Yes, I do, Finn. Everyone does bad stuff."

"Yeah? Like what? Cheating on a test? Getting drunk? I'm talking real shit here."

I stare him down. "So am I."

"Give me one good example." He sets his soda down too hard.

I hesitate.

Finn can't know.

We stand there, looking at each other, like two gunslingers in an old western, and I'm afraid to draw. I imagine a lone tumbleweed blowing across the kitchen.

Finn laughs again, one short, loud, bark. "See, dude? You don't have shit for problems."

I walk slowly to the fridge, take out the mushrooms, and spill them across the chopping board. I stare at them like dregs in the bottom of a tea cup, and Finn sort of huffs and turns away.

"Wait, Finn."

"What?"

I pull a knife from the wooden block. "I know who Xavi hooked up with."

Finn stops cold. "What?"

"Me." I start chopping the mushrooms methodically.

Finn turns back and blinks at me, but doesn't look . . . well, he doesn't even look surprised.

"You're the one that Xavi . . ." He trails off. He tenses, and his football player build looks threatening.

I work hard on the mushrooms, avoiding his eyes.

"Yeah."

"And you care about her, right? You didn't hook up with her just for the bet, did you?" He's still almost hunched, and he has a look on his face like he's concentrating; it's the one he gets when he is actually trying to do homework or something.

I look up, startled. What the hell? Finn knows that I have a thing for my stepsister? "How did you know?"

Finn sort of smirks. "I've known forever, Peter. But it's gotten worse since your dad married her mom and you guys moved in together. You watch her all the time, when you think no one's looking. You make extra of her favorite dishes and put them aside, just in case she might walk in. One day, she said she liked light blue, and suddenly you had eight light-blue shirts."

I swallow. "So it's obvious."

Finn's face goes sort of still and calm, and he shoves his hands in his pockets. "Maybe not to anyone else. At least, no one's said anything, and I think if it were common knowledge that you wanted to get busy with your stepsister, there'd be just a little talk."

"But you know."

Finn glares at me. "I might not get all As, Peter, but I get people. Give me a little credit here."

"Fine. If you're all fucking wise and powerful, then tell me what you need to tell me, Finn. Tell me what's got you acting like such an asshole."

Finn stares at me.

"No." He pauses. "Hurry and get this stuff going. We've got customers out front already."

And Finn grabs his tray and stalks out of the kitchen.

Isa
Wednesday

I stare at the cash in front of me, spread out on the scratched wood of the kitchen table.

Cold, hard cash.

More than from waiting tables.

More than from winning Tips.

And all from just the teensiest, tiniest, most innocent little bit of blackmail.

I could put this in neat little stacks and start to fill a black suitcase. I could put a really great down payment on a damned nice car. While everyone else was risking their neck at dares or working their asses off for high-maintenance customers, Finn was making more money than I could imagine. And he couldn't have actually been spending it. Everything he drove, everything he wore was nice enough, but not *that* nice.

Tips had to seem like nothing to him. Like chump change. Like the stuff you give a particularly efficient bellhop when you're renting the penthouse of a New York City hotel.

But what had he really done with all of it?

"Got the money?" Auntie asks, grinning. She has her normally unkempt hair wound into a careful bun. She's taken the time to put on just a touch of makeup, and she's slipped into her one unscuffed pair of sensible heels.

"Right here." I hold up the stack, and she beams at me like I've just won first prize at the 4-H meeting in the hills.

"I'm sure proud of you, baby girl. I keep telling my friends at bridge I got the most hardest working, talented waitress at Waterside for a niece. Buellah Adler, she said, 'That girl of yours has got to be the best flirt around to be getting all that money,' but I said, 'No, she's just kind and good all the way through to the core.' People see that, you know, Isa. They see it. That's why you're lucky."

My insides twist. "Sure, Auntie. Thank you." Nothing but good waitressing and a little pimping on the side. Or am I a madam? I should have paid more attention to that Heidi Fleiss documentary on HBO.

But maybe I'm just teaching Finn a lesson. Maybe he'll think twice next summer about earning money this way.

Or maybe I'm just selfish.

"Hurry along to the car, now," Auntie says. She pats my head, like I'm a little girl again. "Bring that money and hold onto it real tight, okay?"

I tuck the money into my purse and follow her out to her old Buick. It's beautiful, though. It's one of the only things Auntie still cares about, and even though it's older than I am, there's not a speck of rust to be found on it. Last year when the neighbor boys keyed it, she took it into the shop right away and paid every penny to make it as bright and shiny as new. It was the last thing her husband bought before he died, and he liked to keep his cars as neat as a pin, she liked to say.

She used to have money. Not a lot, but enough. She lived

in a little house in the west part of town with a pretty lawn and a mailbox painted like a chicken coop. But she's kind and my parents knew that, and they never repaid her for her loans. And, if I know anything, they never will.

Auntie sings and clicks her nails on the steering wheel on the way over. I sit quiet, feeling the extra weight in my purse, and stare at the window. At one point, my aunt leans over and puts her hand on my knee. "Aren't you so excited, Isa?" she asks. "I'm just so excited I can barely stand it. I'm glad you got that money. I think it was from God. Don't you think it was from God, Isa?"

"Sure." I look down into my lap. It was funny, though, that I found Finn out and this money all came to me and then this property came onto the market. Very funny. Like it was meant to be.

Or maybe . . . maybe somehow, it's karma. And all the dirty money in the world won't spend my way out of karma. And this place will be in ruins. And we'll never get out of where we are or be people who don't have to adjust the tinfoil on the top of the TV for better reception, like we still live a million years ago, before the Internet.

My aunt pulls up to an old warehouse building, just south of downtown, far away from Waterside. It doesn't necessarily look promising, but sort of charming, in a strange way. Like the dandelions growing up from the little lot next to the building. Or the way the bricks have aged. The strangely placed water spout near the front door.

A shiny black Chevy pickup pulls up in front of the building and stops in the fire lane. A plump, grinning man with hair like aged lace steps and opens his arms to us.

"Ms. Sanchez!" he says. "And this must be your charming niece, Isa?" He grabs my hand so enthusiastically I think he's going to kiss it, but he just shakes it hard and drops it.

"Good afternoon, Mr. Wellsby," my aunt says, grinning. "Thanks for meeting us here."

"Anything for you," he says, his smile still perfectly in place.

Sure, anything for us. Or anything for a commission.

Mr. Wellsby fumbles for a moment in his pocket, and comes out with an overlarge key ring. He clinks through the keys, one by one. "Aha!" he says, holding up a dull brassy key with the number 1212 printed on it. He unlocks the door and swings it open grandly. "Welcome, ladies," he says, "to your brand-new property!"

We walk inside.

It's almost pitch-black.

I stand in the rectangle of light cast by the open door while Mr. Wellsby hums to himself as he feels along the wall for a light switch. A moment later, a harsh fluorescent light flickers weakly in the entryway, and Mr. Wellsby sweeps aside some giant curtains to let more light in.

The place . . . well, it needs work.

The walls are a crumbling red brick and the floors a stained old concrete, chipped in places. A couple of cracks have given way to crawling ivy, nourished by the sunlight coming in through the filmy, overlarge windows.

Most of the industrial light fixtures in the room house jagged, broken lightbulbs, or broken ones where they've burned out. I push open a door in back that leads to a little room that might've been a kitchen once. There are washer and dryer hookups in the corner, and what looks like a faucet that doesn't lead to a sink of any sort. Swinging wooden doors with complaining hinges open to a long hallway that houses bathrooms.

I wander back into the main room. Mr. Wellsby has uncovered a few more windows, revealing the rest of the neglected space.

A large stage juts out from the back, and it looks like someone has broken in and gone all graffiti artist on the back wall. It's beautiful work, bright and stunning, spelling the word "Sun" in oranges and yellows and whites. I could be wrong, but I don't think that's exactly a gang sign. It's sort of perfect.

"That'll need to be painted over, of course," Mr. Wellsby says a bit apologetically. "And of course, there's work to be done here and there in order to make this place, uh, serviceable. But I think we can all agree it's going to be stunning with just a touch of elbow grease."

Maybe a little more than a touch, Mr. Wellsby. But my aunt and I know that. I'm not afraid of work. And if Finn keeps paying me, I could quit my waitressing job and we could have this place in our names, no problem.

Well. In my aunt's name.

Mr. Wellsby toddles happily around the room, pointing out this thing and that. He has the sort of paunch that sticks out like a shelf or something. While he walks, he crosses his hands and rests them on his stomach. "Look at this place!" he says. "Wouldn't these walls be gorgeous in converted loft apartments?"

How much money does he think we have?

"How much are you asking?" Auntie asks. "We aren't rich or nothing."

Nope. Not even close. I pull my purse a little tighter to my side.

Mr. Wellsby puts a pudgy hand on my aunt's shoulders. "Fortunately, Ms. Sanchez, I'm quite taken with you, and I do think we can arrange a deal of sorts. Might you come with me? We can discuss business away from the child's ears."

I snort. A child? Seriously?

"Sure," my aunt says, and Mr. Wellsby offers his arm to her. Mr. Wellsby helps her up the stairs to the stage and draws the ratty red curtains. Even so, I can hear them murmuring.

My aunt is a horrible negotiator. He knows, as well as I do, that the building will be ours in about five seconds at an unfair price.

But it will be ours. And if all goes to plan, we won't be in the trailer much longer.

This crumbling old place—this abandoned warehouse—it's beautiful.

It's perfect. And I want it.

It will make everything worth it.

Finn
Friday

I love working when Isa isn't here.

I actually sort of feel like my old self, I guess. Not to mention Rico's not here, which is always awesome. Josh is working the kitchens, so Peter's taken over the bar, and Xavi's waiting with Warren. It's not a busy day. It's just sort of . . . normal.

I drop off an order in the kitchen and turn around to find Xavi behind me, fidgeting a little. Her face has this sort of greenish color, like she might blow some serious chunks at any moment.

"You okay?" I ask.

She nods. "Yeah. My stepdad has been sick and I think maybe I caught of a touch of it. It's no big deal. It's, like, twenty-four hours of hell and then you're fine. I'm in the final hour, so I should be good. Any second now."

She doesn't look convinced, and she's pretty hunched over.

"Go home," I say. "Make your mom cook you chicken soup."

Xavi shrugs. "I'm fine. And I need the cash. Tips is tomorrow, and I want a little extra."

"Well, let me know if you need something, okay?" I put my hand on her shoulder.

She shrugs away. "Sure. Oh, uh, there's some old dude out front. He's asking for you. Table fourteen."

"Thanks." I glance over at Josh, who seems to be mostly functioning today, and head back out to the floor. I pass Gustavo, who looks flustered. Rico hasn't hired another busgirl to replace Xavi yet. As far as I know, he hasn't even interviewed anyone, even though a bunch of people have applied. I've collected eight applications myself. We were short on bussers anyway, so Gustavo's working overtime and all of the waitstaff have been pitching in. Weird that he hasn't grabbed anyone new. But maybe he doesn't want another interruption with Tips.

I see Mr. Andross before he sees me, and he looks up and lifts his hand.

"Finn!" he says, reaching out to shake my hand. I shift the menu and take his hand. "You look great, buddy. Having a good summer?"

"Yes, sir." I smile. Mr. Andross is the high school principal. "Are you having a great summer?"

He sets his elbows on the table. "Can't complain. Got a pool put in for the girls, so they're happy. Say, how do you think this football season is going to go?"

"Good." And, providing Isa keeps her mouth shut, it will. We're picked as state runners-up in the preseason poll. We came in fourth last year, and my dad's all about winning the whole thing this year. It's why I've been up early, running my ass off every morning.

"Good, son. Say, I didn't really come by to eat, but do you

think maybe you could get me some real breakfast? I don't know much of this French stuff, but if you could cook me up some good old-fashioned scrambled eggs and maybe throw on some bacon, I'd be pretty happy. My wife only has that veggie bacon shit at home and those eggs you pour out of a milk carton." He laughs.

"I'll figure something out for you," I say.

"Oh, and Finn?" Mr. Andross says. He picks up a newspaper from his table. "I grabbed this out of my car for some light breakfast reading, and it's like a year old. Could you toss it for me?"

"No problem." I tuck the newspaper under my arm and head back to the kitchen. On the way back, a woman with an explosion of red-purple hair catches me.

"Can you send Xavi back?" she says. She points at her half-empty Coke.

"Certainly. Just one moment."

In the kitchen I turn to toss the newspaper away, but a picture catches my eye.

Wait a minute. I cock my head to the side and grab the newspaper. Is that—*Isa* on the front page? A very different-looking Isa, with a load of makeup and a dress with all sorts of stones on it. I check the caption.

Isa Sanchez, four-time Miss Moonshine winner, collects scholarship money.

Holy crap. Tough, no-nonsense Isa is a beauty queen? That's like me quitting football and taking up ballet: just plain weird.

I might just be able to use this. I slide it under my street clothes and catch Josh chopping peppers.

"Wanna make something that you'll actually enjoy?" I ask, and he actually grins when I hang up the order.

"Give me a few," he says. "I'll make this guy the best eggs of all time. History-making eggs."

"Sure. Hey, have you seen Xavi? She's not out on the floor. Her customers were asking."

Josh nods toward the staff bathroom. "It's not looking good, dude."

"Thanks, man." I head back and knock on the door. "Xavi?" I ask softly.

Inside, I hear her retch. "I'm fine," she mutters, her voice small.

"You don't sound fine."

She retches again, louder. I try the handle, unsure if I should go in. It's locked.

"Xavi?"

"Just go away," she says. She sounds like she's crying.

"Do you want me to get Peter?"

"No!" she says. She opens the door, holding a paper towel over her mouth. The room reeks of sick. "Don't tell Peter. I don't want to see him."

And then she gags and hurries back to the toilet. "Go away, Finn."

"I'll take your tables, okay?" I say softly. "Just go home. And if you need a ride, I'll take you wherever you need to go."

She nods and pushes her hair back. "Thank you."

I close the door very quietly and fill a new Coke for her table. Fortunately, we weren't crazy busy, and Aida will probably be glad to take any extra tables I can't handle.

I drop the Coke off, check on the other tables, and go back

to Josh, who hands me a gigantic tray of the most gorgeous eggs and bacon I have ever seen. The eggs are fluffy as shit, and the bacon is the perfect sort of crispy.

"Thanks, man," I say. "You got part of my tip if you want it."

"Can't say no to that," Josh says. "We should make this part of the menu, huh?"

I sort of laugh but don't say anything. Even I know that Rico's not going to go for adding Cracker Barrel dishes to the menu.

"This is perfect, Finn," says Mr. Andross as I set the plate in front of him. He grabs his fork eagerly. "I mean, perfect. I should really come in more often."

I put my hands in my pockets and shrug. "Um, well, it's sort of a special. Our cook's really good at this stuff, so, yeah."

He digs in and takes a big forkful of the quivering eggs. "Listen, Finn. I came in here to give you a little something. I know you've got college coming up, and I understand you're concerned about your future, so . . ." He pauses, sets his fork down, and digs into his pocket. He comes out with a leather checkbook. "I'm going to help you out. How does that sound?"

I freeze, right in place, and I stare as Mr. Andross very carefully writes out a four thousand dollar check. He writes my name neatly above the dollar amount. He presses his fingers along the top and, slowly, tears the check out.

He holds it out to me.

"Oh," I say.

"Go ahead," he says, waving it. "Take it."

I stare at the check in his hand. I know what he wants.

The high school principal.

Trying to make a *deal* with me.

Isa's not here. I could get away with saying no.

I look right at him.

Right into his eyes.

I think of Isa and I square my shoulders. "I don't do that anymore, Mr. Andross," I say. "And I wouldn't take a check if I did."

Mr. Andross stares at me for a half minute. "Excuse me?"

Oh shit.

Holy *shit.*

Mr. Andross was actually trying to help me out with college.

He wasn't trying to hire me.

SHIT.

I force a laugh. It's too loud. The Coke woman from Xavi's table looks over, and immediately, like *that fast*, I feel sweat under my collar.

"I can't accept that, Mr. Andross," I say. "I really, really appreciate it. And I think it's great. But my dad works too hard for me to accept it. I don't think he'd like it."

Mr. Andross just sits here, his eyes big, and the check still dangling from his fingers. "I would've taken care of everything with your dad, you know."

I'm not sure of that. But I laugh again. "I didn't make a good joke, huh?"

Is he buying it? I can't tell. He has to buy it.

Sweat crawls along my hairline.

Mr. Andross puts the check carefully back into his checkbook and leans forward to slip it into his back pocket. "Not really, Finn."

Xavi
Sunday
3:00 a.m.

I take a sip of my beer.

It's gotten warm.

It's still my first beer tonight. First beer at Tips. Everyone else is pretty much wasted. Trashed. Aida and Jeremiah are making out instead of listening to Rico, who is trying to gather more money.

"Think we should up the buy-in, Triple X?" Rico says, nudging me. "Think we should ask for more? Make the game elite?"

I think of Celia and Jake and Gustavo.

"No."

I don't have the energy to argue with him about my name.

I take another quick drink. It doesn't go down easy. My stomach churns like I've swallowed a damn KitchenAid mixer or something, I don't know. But I feel like shit. This flu stuff was supposed to go away. I press my hand to my stomach.

It's not like it's something other than the flu.

It's not.

Rico holds up his hands. "Ladies and gentleman, it's time for Tips! All entries, please stand!"

I push myself up and sway slightly. Peter, who has been sitting across from me all night, extracts himself and comes to stand beside me.

"You okay?" he asks. I sway a little farther, and he puts his hand on my arm, steadying me. "Xavi, are you drunk?"

I shake my head and set my beer down on the ground. "I feel . . . weird," I say. "Really, really, weird."

"Do you want to go home? I've hardly had anything. I can drive if you give me a minute or so."

I look up at him. "No. I have to stay. I have to try to win."

It's all about winning.

It's not about what's going on with my body. It's not about me ruining my life.

It's about Tips.

Peter wraps his arms around me, right there in front of everyone. "Okay," he says. "Then, can I stay with you? Make sure you're okay?"

I want to push him away, tell him I am just fine by myself, but I close my eyes tight and nod into his shirt. "Okay."

"Tonight," Rico says, "tonight, we have a very special daremaker. And that person is a longtime Tips champ, Finn!"

Holy shit. Finn actually showed up. I didn't even see him arrive.

Finn doesn't smile. He just downs the rest of his beer. "The dare is, you have to swipe Chief Surgeon Li's keys next time he comes to the restaurant. And you have to hold on to them for three solid days before you let him find them."

"Do you want to stay standing?" Peter murmurs into my hair.

I nod, clinging to him. "I'm in," I say. "I earned it."

Peter frowns down at me. "What do you mean 'you earned it'?"

Oh my damn. Peter is totally going to find out what I did. He can't. He might hate me until, like, the zombie apocalypse, and I can't even deal with him hating me right now.

"I earned the money," I whisper. "It's the best I can do right now."

Finn steps up closer to the whimpering bonfire. Peter stays standing beside me, and Aida, Warren, Jeremiah, and even Gustavo show up. And he's standing. Isa stands too, her fingers tangled in her hair. Jake's not playing tonight, and neither is Celia or Josh. They're back from the fire, giggling and drinking and having a billion times more fun than I am.

I pull a bill out of my pocket—I scribbled my initials on it earlier—and drop it into the hat that Gustavo shoves at me. Gustavo rushes it back to Finn, who reaches inside.

"Isa," he reads, his voice dull.

Isa pulls a ridiculous grin and raises an arm, pointing directly at Finn with this weird, taunting glory in her eyes. "I'll take that bet, Finn!" she shouts, and then grabs a bottle of vodka and downs a couple of shots. "And I'll win!"

I tug on Peter's arm.

"What is it?" he asks.

"I need you to take me downstairs," I say, my stomach lurching. "I'm going to be sick."

Peter helps me toward the ladder and climbs down first so he can catch me if I fall. Oh my damn, he is the sweetest guy ever. I am going to die if . . . if this is screwed up. If we screwed it up. I mean, it takes two. But I can't be mad at him. I can't.

I grab the rungs of the ladder and lower myself carefully downward.

"Take it slow," Peter advises from below. "One rung at a time."

I look down and see him below me, his hands outstretched in case I fall. Suddenly I feel crazy dizzy. Like I just took fourteen shots and jumped on a trampoline dizzy. I press my forehead against a metal rung and hold on as tight as I can.

"It's okay, Xavi," Peter whispers.

I slowly drop my hand to cling to the next rung, and then my foot follows. And then I repeat it, but my head swims, and my stomach makes this strange, growling noise.

I do the rest quickly, my feet slipping down the rungs, and jump off when I get close to the floor, landing clumsily. I stumble, but Peter catches me.

And then it happens.

My stomach surges, and I vomit, all over Rico's scratched-up desk. Across the papers and the horseshoe game and a stack of manila envelopes.

Suddenly with my cookies tossed and my feet firmly on the ground, I feel better. *Way* better. Better enough to feel, like, Mira Ellston levels of embarrassment, when she farted really loudly while she was doing equations on the marker board. Or like Emery Smith, who fell on his face at a school assembly when his pants came down.

Except so, so much worse.

Peter doesn't say anything. Instead, he just disappears, and comes back a moment later with a thick roll of paper towels, a pan of water, and a small bottle of dish soap. He hands me a paper towel and I wipe off my face and the little bits of vomit clinging to my hair, and he starts working on Rico's desk, swiping the sick away and pushing it into the trashcan like he is some sort of puke superhero and it doesn't even bother him.

I almost throw up again. "Peter, no," I croak, but my voice is hoarse from puking my guts out.

He gives me a quick smile. "Don't worry about it, Xavi. You think I haven't done this before? I pick up the late shift at the bar a lot, after the kitchen closes and Rico goes home, when all the townies come in and get smashed on cocktails and stumble out. Trust me—I'm a pro."

He tosses the documents into the trash, and then pulls the papers out of the wet manila folder and lays them, face-down, on the desk. "Huh," he says. "Looks like Rico's not keeping up with his bills very well."

Feeling a little nosy, I pick them up. Past due: electricity. Past due: car payment. Past due: television. "Why the hell isn't Rico paying these?" I ask. "Does General Steakhouse have us in that bad shape?"

Peter shakes his head. "They shouldn't. Our nights are still crazy busy. He scratches his hair. "You know when I did that article? The reporter said we were one of the highest-grossing restaurants in the region. There's no way we should be in trouble like that." He takes the papers from my hands and tosses them back onto the desk . . . just in time for my stomach to go roller coaster on me again. Oh no.

I put my hand over my mouth and sprint off to the staff bathroom.

Peter follows and holds my hair back while I vomit. I clean

my mouth off with a little square of toilet tissue and stare into the mirror. I look like an early twenties celeb right before a stint in rehab. I look like I'm half dead.

Peter wraps me in his arms and holds me to his chest. "Xavi," he says. "How long has this been going on?"

I bury my face in his neck. "Too long, Peter."

He strokes my hair slowly, for a long time, and whispers sweet little things into my ear. I let him. How weird that the person who I was avoiding is the same person who gives me the most comfort? That he's the only person I want to be with right now?

"Xavi," he says finally.

"Yeah?" I tilt my face up, and he shifts back, just a tiny bit, probably because my breath smells like roadkill.

"I'm going to take you home."

Peter
Sunday
4:24 a.m.

Xavi is slumped over in my front seat, her hair messily tied back with a hair band one of my ex-girlfriend's slipped around my gear shift a few months ago, when I'd been dating to date and thinking about my stepsister with every kiss.

It sounds wrong when I say it like that.

And maybe it is wrong.

Xavi shifts slightly and presses her forehead to the glass of the passenger-side window.

"You cool?" I ask. "If you need me to pull over, I can pull over."

She mumbles something, but she doesn't make any sudden movements, so I keep driving, trying to keep my braking gentle and my turns wide and slow. There aren't many people on the road at this hour, fortunately.

I sigh heavily and watch my lane switch to gravel as I turn toward the country, away from the noises and lights of the city. This isn't how I wanted it to be with Xavi. I wanted to really be with her. I wanted to listen to her talk about all the stuff that she wanted. I wanted to take her on a real date—one where we went to an actual restaurant and ordered food and I'd pay the check at the end. I wanted to open doors for her and walk on the outside of the sidewalk and kiss her for no reason.

I know that sounds lame, but I liked her like that. I liked her a lot. If the guys knew, they'd call me whipped and laugh, but I don't give a shit.

I didn't want to be like this. I wanted the stolen kiss on the roof of the shed, not our first hookup on the floor of the bar. I look over at her, the way she's sitting—with her red face against the glass, her eyes squeezed shut, and her other hand on her stomach.

Holy mother of . . .

Is she *pregnant*?

If she's pregnant, isn't throwing up something that's supposed to only happen in the mornings? But what if . . . what if I messed up big time?

We didn't use protection or anything. It just . . . happened.

Fuck.

My dad would kill me. I'd lose everything. I would have to stay here and attend community college and work. I'd never go to school for IT, like my dad wants. I'd never become a world-renowned chef, like Dubois.

I'd be Peter, Teenage Daddy, who hooked up with his stepsister.

Forever.

I've seen *Teenage Mom*, or whatever, on MTV. I know this shit never actually works out.

Xavi moves her head. Part of her hair comes loose from the band and falls down her shoulders. She is beautiful, though, even when she's sick and her makeup is half rubbed off. She's stunning.

I pull into the driveway and watch her for a moment. She stays still and slumped until she realizes the car is off, and then she looks sleepily up at me, blinking hard. "We home?" she asks.

I nod and help her take off her seat belt. I open the driver's-side door and help her out and into the house. She kind of jumps when I wrap an arm under her to keep her steady, but lets me ease the door open and guide her into her bedroom. I set her carefully on her bed.

"Stay," she whispers, her fingers pulling at my leg. "Stay with me."

That's a bad idea. I know that's a bad idea. "I'll sit with you until you go to sleep." She's lying on top of her covers, so I pull a throw off her computer chair and tuck it around her so she stays warm.

"Peter?" she whispers.

"Yeah?" I smooth the hair away from her forehead. It's sticky with sweat. Maybe I should get her mom.

But no—if Xavi's knocked up, her mom's the last one who needs to know right now.

"You're nice."

I smile a little, in spite of everything. And Xavi falls asleep, her mouth a little open.

I get up and pull the trash can close, in case she gets sick again, and pour her a glass of water from the bathroom tap for her nightstand. I grab a soft towel from under the sink and leave it next to her pillow—just in case.

Then I leave her. If either of our parents found us together this late at night . . . well . . . they might assume things.

I sit in my room with a glass of bourbon I borrowed from

my dad's bar. If there is one thing he knows how to do, it's buy good alcohol. And he's not really stingy with it either. As long as I'm not being a dumbass, he doesn't mind if I have a glass every now and then.

I turn the glass in my hand. My fingers leave streaks in the condensation, where the ice is melting into the liquor. I wonder what would happen if I offered the drink to Xavi. All night, she nursed one beer. One, single beer. And she didn't even half finish it. I know, because I watched. Unless she drank a ton before she got there, but she didn't seem drunk. She wasn't.

I stand up and open my window, then crawl out onto the sloping garage roof to finish my drink. I'd rather be in the open pasture right now, but I've had enough that I shouldn't drive out there.

If I offered the bourbon to Xavi, would she take it? Or would she have to say no?

Maybe this was all a mistake. Maybe falling in love with Xavi Diane Mitchell wasn't such a bright move.

For a second, I want to run. To get out. To start fresh, away from my dad and Xavi and everyone.

But what's done is done.

Isa
Tuesday

"Here," Finn says, shoving a thick white envelope into my hands. "Take it. Hurry."

It's just after four thirty, so the restaurant is basically empty. I look left and right. The woman in the corner is too busy enjoying her seventh glass of Chardonnay to worry about a little cash, and the other two tables are on the other side of the bar. But the evening rush is about to start. I ease open the envelope and stare inside.

"Holy shit, Finn," I say. "There's more money in here than last week."

Finn looks really unhappy. "Yeah," he says. "Whatever." He frowns, looking super pissed. But I don't care.

This is *amazing*. This will make payments for the next three months on the warehouse. Not counting my tips, and what I'll get from winning.

Damn, do I ever love money. I grin. "We make a great team, don't we?"

He stares at me, and his eyes are arctic cold. "I wouldn't call it a team, Isa," he spits, and stalks off, leaving me with the heavy envelope.

I tuck it into my cummerbund and head out to my car, where I stash it under the floor mat. I lock the doors tight and put my keys back in my purse under a chair in the kitchen. We've never had a theft incident at Waterside, but you can't be too careful.

I laugh a little gleefully to myself. Peter's on tonight, and he's already hard at work on tonight's specials—a rich bouillabaisse is simmering on the stove, and he's preparing the escargot now. I'm not particularly into snail, but anytime Peter makes them, we get absolutely slammed. Jeremiah's supposed to be here in an hour, and if Xavi feels okay, she'll be in to help too. I can't imagine Aida would say no if we ended up needing her tonight.

Peter flashes me a quick grin and Jake blows soap bubbles at me, which I dodge with a giggle.

For once in my life, everything seems pretty great.

"Guess who just wandered in?" Jake asks.

"Who?" I frown. It couldn't be the Witch.

"Chief Surgeon Li," Jake says with a devilish sort of grin. "You're on, Isa. Let's see what you've got."

I toss my hair and smile. Chief Surgeon Li is commonly known as one of the city's most eligible bachelors. Or he was until it became clear he probably wasn't ever going to get married. Women love him, guys worship him, and Finn probably thought any girl would have a lot of trouble doing anything mean to someone as great as Chief Surgeon Li. But I've seen the chief surgeon here before, and I have a plan.

I run into the bathroom to check my reflection and then I head out to the floor. Li has already been seated, but this is my table. Everyone knows it's my table.

I paste on my most professional look for the chief surgeon and his guest. Well, maybe his girlfriend, at least for today. She's beautiful, with long blond hair and a dress that has less fabric than my entire shirt. She also has a smile that's fixed very carefully in place. She knows what she's doing.

"Dr. Li!" I say. "How are you this lovely evening?"

Dr. Li considers me. "I'm doing well. Isa, isn't it?"

Damn it. It would all be easier if he didn't know who I was. But that's Li for you. An eye for anything female in a fifty-mile radius.

"Yes. Have you had a chance to look at our drinks menu?" I glance over at the bar. Rico's back.

"Yes, Isa. Could I get, uh, a scotch, please? Your finest? On the rocks?"

"Certainly. And you, miss?" I take a wild guess, assuming she's not married and/or doesn't prefer the term "ma'am."

"Hmm. Strawberry margarita. Blended, please." She points at the menu.

"I'll have those right up. Dr. Li, it's pretty warm in here. Would you care for me to check your jacket to our coat closet?" I ask as I pass them the dinner menus. Dr. Li is wearing an expensive suit that's way too warm for dinner in the summer. Still, a lot of our male patrons do it. Apparently, a jacket that screams *I have mountains of disposable income* is never out of season.

Dr. Li smiles warmly at me, and the blonde across the table bristles slightly but doesn't say anything. "Please, Isa." He shrugs out of his coat and hands it to me. I snag a napkin from the hostess podium and take the jacket back to the coat room. I hide in the deepest corner and slip my hand inside his pocket.

Jackpot.

I pull out the keys, wrap them in a napkin to get rid of the jangle, and slip them down my shirt, then I head back to the bar. Rico gives me a mischievous grin, but I ignore him. "Could you get a strawberry margarita and our finest scotch for Dr. Li's table?"

Rico nods and then points at the door. About ten people have arrived, all at once.

"Get Finn out here. Stat." I head back to the kitchen, half thankful he didn't expect me to serve them. I hurry out the back door and hide the keys, napkin and all, under the floor mat in my car, next to the money, and then find Finn on the back patio.

"Done and done," I say, wiping my hands gleefully.

"Good for you." Finn doesn't look at me. "Aren't you just becoming quite the little businesswoman?"

I ignore his shitty tone. "Rico wants you inside. The dinner rush is starting."

Finn doesn't say anything. He just looks at me for a minute and heads back inside, letting the screen door slam after him.

I guess I should help. Even Finn's not good enough to handle everyone. Thank God. There's going to be enough jackets checked that one little missing set of keys isn't going to be a big deal.

I hope.

Rico's waiting for me in the kitchen, like he didn't expect me to be able to fetch Finn all by my lonesome.

"What?" I ask. He shakes his head, and I follow him back out to the bar to grab Chief Surgeon Li and his date their drinks. "Have you had a chance to look at the menu?" I ask. "Our specials tonight are Dubois's signature bouillabaisse and escargot."

"I'll take the escargot. And I don't suppose you're making any éclairs tonight?" the woman asks. "Éclairs are my absolute favorite. I would *bathe* in them. Wouldn't I bathe in them, darling?"

"She would bathe in them," Dr. Li agrees.

Peter's cooking. He can figure it out. "Of course we can." I make a note on the order.

"And I'll have both specials. And perhaps a half order of the croissants? If I remember correctly, your chef makes excellent croissants." He winks at his date.

"Absolutely. Anything else? Any appetizers?"

"No thank you, Isa, but you've been wonderful. Thank you."

Sheesh. Of course this guy lays it on thick now, after I've stolen his keys. It's like he knows. Like he's looking into my eyes and actually *knows* that I have his keys.

Part of me wants to call it off. To sneak his keys back into his pocket and return them to him without incident. But I can't. Besides, there couldn't be a better night. More people just walked in the door.

Xavi comes out, looking all perky and professional in her starchy new uniform. She sees who I'm waiting on and grins at me. I give her a thumbs-up as I pass her on my way to the front to seat new guests, and she mouths, "I knew you could do it."

The night gets so busy I half forget I've stolen the chief surgeon's keys at all. I drop the check off by their table—a big check, I might add, as I've been feeding them drinks all night, and they're both drunk as hell.

"Chief Surgeon Li," I ask. "Would you like Raj to call you a cab?"

The chief surgeon grins at me. "What, Isa? Concerned for my well-being? I'm touched. You're a fantastic waitress. You know, I think that would be great. What do you think, Lea?" he asks, addressing the woman across the table.

She hiccups and puts a hand over her mouth. "Probably for the best." She gives me a thankful smile.

I head outside and ask Raj to call a cab for Doctor Li. Raj makes a face. "That man won't let me valet his car and now he wants a cab?" He makes a disgusted noise in his throat.

I try not to smile. I know Raj just wants to have a quick spin in the doctor's Bentley. I leave him to it and walk back to the floor, and to the coat closet. I take Chief Surgeon Li's suit jacket off the hanger, put it neatly over my arm, and head back to his table.

"Thanks, Isa," Dr. Li says as he slips it on.

"Your cab will be here shortly." My hands are sweating. My face has to be red right now. Is my face red? Please, please don't let him check his pockets. Don't let him realize they're empty.

He slides his hand into his pocket.

Oh, holy shit.

I am screwed.

But then the doctor just holds his arm out to his date, Lea, and they stroll out of the restaurant, leaving me with my bazillion other tables to deal with.

I ignore my other customers for five seconds and head back to the kitchen, where I flop down on a crappy metal chair that Peter dragged in here for breaks. My car keys have fallen out of my purse, which I had stashed under the chair earlier, and are lying on the floor.

"How'd it go?" Peter asks. He tosses me an extra éclair. I catch it and take a bite.

"Honestly?" I ask, my heart beating at a machine gun staccato, "it couldn't have been better."

Finn
Wednesday

"What the hell kind of move was that, Finn?" my dad asks, his nostrils flaring. "That sort of joke? With the high school principal? Really?" His hands are balled into fists and there's a spot on his T-shirt where he spilled purple Gatorade.

I don't look directly at him. Instead I focus on the screen behind him, where some pretty woman is trying to sell a blender. "He knew I was kidding, Dad."

"He might have known you were kidding, but he sure as hell didn't think it was funny!" Dad roars. "What kind of bullshit move was that?" He grabs the remote and turns off the television.

"Sorry," I grunt. I look back toward my room. I have to work in thirty minutes . . . but the way my dad's going, I'm probably not going to get out of here for another hour. You'd think I lost a football game or something.

"And you might as well have just thrown the money back in his face, Finn!" Dad roars.

"I didn't think you'd want me accepting his charity!" I say, pushing myself out of his chair. "What was I supposed to do? I was trying to get out of it gracefully."

"You would have been more graceful if you'd punched him!" Dad says, getting right up in my face. "And you're right—I didn't want you taking the money. But you made some strange joke to the guy who signs my paycheck? The man who is the lay leader every weekend at the Baptist church? You were trying to be *funny*?"

"I'm sorry," I say, looking down.

And he has no idea how sorry I actually am. No idea.

"Bullshit," he snarls. "You're grounded. Until school starts."

"Yes, sir."

He won't ground me. He doesn't keep close enough track to do it. But the threat shows how completely pissed he is.

He stands there, huffing and puffing at me, his face a shade of red I've only seen in cartoons, right before someone's head blows up.

"Uh, Dad?"

"What?" he asks.

"I have to, uh . . . go to work."

"Then get to work. And get your ass straight back here after." His voice has lowered to a growl. I can't remember the last time I've seen him this pissed—maybe when the Trowski brothers showed up to practice smashed the day before a game. *That* was really bad.

I head to my room to grab my uniform. I slip my wallet into my pocket—and then I stop at my desk and grab the clipping about Isa. The one from the newspaper that Mr. Andross gave me. The one that reveals her as a "pageant princess."

Something tells me she won't want this getting out. So maybe I can use it for leverage.

Or maybe I'm totally wrong, and she won't give a shit.

I slide the clipping into my back pocket and crawl out my window. There's no point even risking walking past my dad again, even though I hear the TV turn back on in the living room.

Twelve minutes later, I pull up to the restaurant, and there's someone there.

Someone who's usually not.

Holy shit. Holy *shit*.

My hands shake on my steering wheel. I grip it tighter.

There is a cop car parked outside of the Waterside Café.

And there's only one reason I can think of why there would be a cop car parked outside the Waterside Café.

Because of me.

Because maybe Isa told, or Elaine Carpenter snapped when I ditched her, or something. Maybe one of my other clients got jealous, or maybe . . . who the hell knows?

They know.

I drive a circle around the restaurant and head into the trees and park where my car isn't visible. Then I call Isa.

She doesn't answer.

I hang up fast. Crap. Maybe I shouldn't have called her. Maybe she's with the police *right now*, and she's giving them my address.

Maybe they're already there. Maybe they sent one car to work and another one to my house to cover all of their bases or something.

My father's head will literally explode.

My phone rings in my hand, and I about jump out of my seat. It's Isa.

I'm not answering.

No freaking way am I answering.

I stare at the phone.

"Hello?" I say.

"Finn," Isa says. "What's up? Got more money for me?"

The way she says it is teasing and horrible. I can't believe I had feelings for her. I can't believe I took her on a date. I would've had a better time with Gustavo the busboy.

"No," I say. "I have to stop. The cops are onto me. It's over, Isa."

She pauses for a long time. "What makes you say that?"

Even though there's no one in the car with me, I lower my voice and cup my hand around the phone.

"The cops are at Waterside *right now*," I whisper.

"Um, what? I can hardly hear you, Finn."

"The cops are at Waterside! Right now!"

"Where?" Isa asks.

"Parked right in front of the building! Why the hell else would they be there?"

Isa pauses again. "Finn?" she says, finally.

"What?"

"They're eating here. For lunch. That's all."

"They're eating?"

"That's what people do in restaurants, Finn." She sounds bored with me. "Rico says to get your ass here. Your shift started ten minutes ago."

She hangs up.

I sit in my car.

They're eating.

Just *eating*.

I am an idiot.

I drive out of the trees and park in my normal spot behind the building.

Deep inside, some part of me is disappointed. Because I don't want anything more—not college, or a girlfriend, or a boyfriend, or Isa—more than I want to stop.

Xavi
Thursday

Yesterday I felt okay and everything was okay and I was all, okay.

And now, I am *definitely not okay.*

I'm, like, the opposite of okay.

Because I look super fat today. And not in the stupid teenage girl way, where we've been brainwashed by fashion magazines to believe we all have to be these perfect airbrushed models. I mean that when I turn sideways and look in the mirror, I can practically see a *baby.* Like, it's very obvious I have a bump there. And it's very obvious that it's because I'm now responsible for another human life.

I haven't taken a test, but I *know.* I can see it.

I touch my hand to my stomach.

And someone snaps, right in front of my face.

"Xavi!" Isa says. "What are you doing? Are you okay? Are you feeling sick?" Isa nods down to my hand, which is still resting on my baby bump.

Damn. I just called it a baby bump.

Please, if someone could just kill me now. I would totally pay for it. I would put a hit out on myself. I would give them all of my Tips money. What will I design now? Onesies and maybe a tiny toddler shoe line? Yeah. No thanks.

"I'm fine," I say, smiling as big as I can.

Isa frowns at me. Her arms are crossed tight over her chest, and one finger is tap-tapping against her other arm. "You know, if there's something going on, I'm here for you. I mean, we can talk about it. I'm a pretty decent listener."

Sure she is. She'd just love to hear how I got knocked up by my stepbrother on the floor of the bar. Maybe we could paint our toenails and she could help me fill out my application for *16 and Pregnant*.

"I'll keep that in mind, Isa, thanks."

She just stands there and sort of stares at me, like she's expecting me to throw up all of my emotions on the floor of the kitchen.

"Um," I say. "Customers."

I head out to the tables, praying someone has come in so I can avoid Isa.

And someone's here.

Chief Surgeon Li is here.

I turn around and walk back into the kitchen. "Isa," I say, "whatever you do, do not go out onto the floor."

"Why?" she asks.

I hold my hand up to stop her. "Just don't."

She totally ignores me and peeks out through the double doors. She turns back to me, her face pale. "Oh my gosh, Xavi. I cannot go out there."

"Hey, Isa," I hiss. "Remember when I said, 'Whatever you do, do not go out onto the floor?'"

She shoots me a look. "What am I supposed to do?"

"Just stay back here. Go hide in the bathroom. I'll take care of him."

"Take care of him?" Isa asks, her eyes wide. "What are you going to do to him?"

I have always disliked people who roll their eyes, but I roll my eyes anyway. "I'm going to stuff him in my trunk and feed him acid. Nothing! Just go."

Isa takes off toward the bathroom and I head out to the floor.

"Dr. Li!" I say. "Back so soon? Table for one?"

Dr. Li smiles at me. "No, Xavi. Not today. Actually, I finally came back to get my car, but I can't find my keys anywhere."

"Oh no!" I say, trying for visibly shaken. I put my hand on my chest and everything. "Do you have a spare set?"

He holds up a key ring and sort of swings it around his finger. "I had one made this morning. I just wanted to see if anyone had turned some in? I had a rather good time, so I don't remember it all. I know I brought them in. And I know I left in a taxi."

"Hmm." I press a finger to my lips, like I'm thinking hard. "I don't think anyone has turned anything in. Unless you are missing a Boba Fett action figure wearing high heels, but I think that belongs to Peter. Did you try calling the taxi service? Maybe they found them?"

"Yeah," Dr. Li says. "Would you mind if I just looked around?"

"Good idea. Did you have them with you at the table?"

Dr. Li shrugs, and then snaps his fingers. "Oh. *Oh.* Maybe they fell out in the coat closet. Could you check?"

"Of course."

I walk over into the coat closet and actually check the floor, like they might really be there. This is some serious method acting I am doing right now. "No dice," I call as I come out, and Dr. Li stops poking around the table.

"I'm just worried they were stolen and I didn't notice," Dr. Li says. "Teach me to go easy on the scotch, huh?"

I pat Dr. Li on the arm. "I'm sure they'll show up."

He grins at me in this exceptionally charming way. "Thanks for your help, Xavi. Hey, tell that other waitress I said hi, huh?"

I nod. "Sure." Flattering. He thinks Isa's name is "that other waitress."

He gives me this cute little salute and heads toward the door.

"Hope you find your keys," I say as he leaves.

Isa comes out a half second later. Obviously she had not gone into the bathroom, like I suggested. "That was freaking close," she says, breathing out. "You were good."

"If you're saying I deserve a freaking Academy Award, then you're right." I toss my hair. "I'm going to make my Oscar speech now, and . . ." I pause, trailing off.

"And what?" Isa giggles.

"Nothing." I feel the hard pit return to my heart.

Isa puts her hand on my shoulder, but I pull away.

For just a few minutes, I forgot that I'm pregnant.

Peter
Friday

Whenever I play that stupid two truths and a lie game, I always tell three lies.

I think whatever people choose to believe says a lot about them. Or maybe it just says I'm a liar. I guess I don't really care.

But for some reason, 40 percent of teachers, and like, 200 percent of camp counselors seem to think that stupid game is a great idea.

I wonder what I'd say now. Maybe I'd tell three truths.

I got a girl pregnant. I'm in love with my stepsister. I hate my life.

Which one would people choose not to believe?

They all pretty much suck.

I wish I wasn't in love with Xavi. I wish I could look at this dispassionately. Make a decision. I don't want to like her.

I'm pouring drinks today. I miss the peace of the kitchen. I miss not having to be *on* all the time. But Rico's completely certain that Josh needs the extra experience around times that aren't exactly peak, so I'm stuck at the bar, watching Rico chum around stupidly with fat men in expensive suits.

Worse, Rico's right about Josh. The guy needs some

serious practice if he's going to make it here, or he might spontaneously combust.

I glance over at Rico. What the hell is he doing now? He has a stack of something in his hands, and he keeps fanning them out like playing cards.

One of the fat men makes a grab for them, and Rico pulls them away.

One of them flutters to the ground. No one notices.

A couple minutes later, one of the men stands up and follows Rico back into the kitchen. What the hell? Rico never brings customers into the kitchen. Especially not when Josh is cooking.

The other guy just sort of sits there and then, disgustedly, he throws his napkin on the table and stalks out of the restaurant, his face pink.

I look back at the kitchen, then dart out from behind the bar to pick up the card.

It's a photo—an old-fashioned Polaroid type.

I flip it over.

Fuck.

It's of a naked girl. A completely, 100 percent naked girl.

And that naked girl is Xavi.

It's *Xavi*.

Even though the top half of her head is cut off, I can tell. I can see it in the pink of her lower lip and the stubborn jut of her chin. I would know her body anywhere, just from the one time. I recognize the little mole on her hip and the curve of her stomach. I *know* her.

My hands start to shake.

I'm going to kill Rico.

I am actually going to tear him to pieces like confetti.

That fucking *pedophile*.

I crumple the picture in my hand and stomp back to the kitchen. "Where's Rico?" I ask Josh. He points at Rico's office. The door is closed.

I tear it open, and Rico's in there with the fat man, pictures spread out over his desk. I recognize a few of Xavi right away, but there are so, so many more. Girls I recognize. Girls who used to work here. Girls who *do* work here.

Rico freezes and looks up at me.

"I should go," the man says, and squeezes past me, his belly bumping me on the way out. I don't move.

"What in the hell is this, Rico?" I ask. I ball up my fists at my sides and take a deep breath, forcing myself to be calm. "Why do you have these pictures? And why are you showing them to people?"

Rico stares at me, and a decrepit smile creeps over his face. "Do you want to see them, Peter?" he asks. "Take home a few as souvenirs? I don't mind, you know. All I ask for is your silence." He snickers a little bit.

"I think I'm going to take all of them, actually."

Keep it together, Peter. Keep it together. Do not go ballistic on this guy.

I take another deep, slow breath.

"I don't think I'm going to let you do that," Rico says. "What if I want to enjoy a moment alone with the help of your stepsister?"

I deck him. My fist connects with his eye socket, and then I pull back and hit him on the chin, as hard as I can.

He goes down. Hard.

"Stay down, asshole, if you don't want me to call the cops." I push all of the pictures into a pile and throw them into a manila envelope sitting on the desk. Rico sputters on the floor, and a dribble of blood comes out of his mouth.

"You're fucking fired," he says, lifting his head slightly.

I glare at him. "No, I'm not. And if you ever try to fire me again, I'm showing these to the cops. They have your finger-prints all over them, you lowlife asswipe." I seal the envelope. "Stay on the floor. I'm leaving early today. You can figure your shit out and take over the bar. But if I find you with one more goddamned picture, I will beat your ass so hard you'll never see straight again."

Rico swallows noisily and stares up at me.

I tuck the pictures under my arm. I'm going to burn them when I get home, but he doesn't need to know that. I should go to the police, but then our parents would get involved, and the parents of the other girls, and word would get out . . . and Xavi doesn't need any attention right now.

"Pete . . . buddy . . . ," he says. His eye is already swelling.

"Fuck off."

I spit on him and walk out.

Isa
Sunday

Today is the day I get to "find" the chief surgeon's keys.

I grin. I'm going to get away with this whole thing. This is the only actual illegal dare I've ever heard of—although I guess the streaking dares are kind of illegal, and yeah, Finn probably could have been arrested for his banana hammock . . . but this was serious.

And I pulled it off.

It's a crazy, wonderful night here. Most of the diners are actually gone, and the remaining ones just want to drink. They're happy and laughing. I feel like I've caught some of their buzz, because I'm happy too.

Rico gave me the cash for winning the dare today. My great-aunt's going to be so thrilled with me. And with the income from Finn, I could quit Waterside. Of course, I need it as a cover, and sure, during the school year my great-aunt's going to have to pony up a little more, but if all goes well, then she won't have to do much. And pretty soon it'll start paying for itself.

I'm done with the embarrassment of pageants forever.

I'm done supporting my parents.

Life is pretty awesome.

I walk outside and spend a moment in the night air. Peter has the radio turned way up in the kitchen while he cleans up, and an old Zeppelin song floats out. I smile and look up. The stars are out and the moon is half-full, light enough to make the night perfect for a walk. Crickets are playing their insistent music, and frogs are singing along the shoreline.

Inside, the Zeppelin song ends. The news begins, and I half listen. The smell of cigarette smoke floats up from the shoreline, and a newswoman's voice comes from the open window in the kitchen.

"Reportedly, a home on North Arapahoe Drive was robbed earlier this evening, with several thousand dollars of possessions stolen. Early reports say the house belongs to Chief Surgeon Alan Li, a beloved member of our community. Li reported losing his keys a few days earlier after a night out. Police are currently on the scene."

What? Did I just hear . . . What?

I run inside and grab my keys, and then sprint out to my car. I unlock it quickly and lift the floor mat.

The keys are still there, wrapped carefully in a napkin. Like they'd never left.

So who broke into the house?

Peter comes sprinting out from the kitchen. "Isa, did you just hear that shit? Tell me you just heard that shit."

I nod. My heart beats so hard I think it's going to crack my ribs. "I heard it."

"You didn't . . . ?"

"Of course not, Peter!" I lift my floor mat again, so he can see the doctor's key ring. "I haven't moved them, I swear to God. I swear to God."

"Calm down." He holds his hands up. "Now think. Are you sure this is exactly where you left them? They haven't moved?"

I lift the floor mat again. "Um, maybe."

Actually, I think they have. I'd thrown them in a little close to the gas pedals, to make sure I didn't accidentally kick them out. Still, they could have slipped down, right? I didn't anchor them in place or anything.

But . . . when I'd come back from finishing up with Dr. Li's table, *my* keys had been in a different place. I'd just thought they'd fallen out of my purse, but what if they hadn't?

Peter grabs my shoulders. "Listen, Isa. You need to hide these, and you need to hide them now."

I shake my head. "But wouldn't it clear me? If I turned them in and, like, someone else's fingerprints are on them? I can't keep them, Peter. I have to go to the police."

"No," Peter says. "You stole the keys. You've just aided in a real crime, whether you wanted to or not. Hide them. Now."

I nod. "Okay."

Peter releases me, and I hurry inside and run into the bathroom, slamming the door behind me. I pull out the keys, still bundled in the napkin. The last thing I need is to get fingerprints on them. My heart is in my throat and I feel like I'm going to choke. How could everything have gone so horribly freaking wrong? One stupid prank and suddenly I could be at fault for robbery?

I can't even—I can't process it.

I would never do that.

Maybe this is karma. Maybe this is my payback for being such a huge bitch to Finn. Maybe this is, like, God telling me that I am a sucky person.

He would be right. I am a sucky person.

I climb up on the toilet, push a ceiling tile upward, and slide the keys up inside. I run outside, grab a roll of duct tape from Rico's office, and tape them to one of the little metal things running across the ceiling, so someone would actually have to get up there to find them. They couldn't just lift a ceiling tile and have them fall down.

I'm so stupid. Why would I do that? And why would I do that to Chief Surgeon Li, whom everyone loves?

Maybe they'll think an angry lover did it. It would make more sense.

I step off the toilet and open the door.

And standing right there, right in front of me, is a super angry Rico. A big purple bruise is blooming on his cheek, and his left eye is swollen completely shut.

"My office," he growls. "Right now."

Finn
Friday

"I quit," Isa screeches at Rico. "I quit this stupid job and this stupid restaurant and your creepy ass games."

Her voice is loud, even through the closed door.

I flatten myself against the wall outside Rico's office. I'm normally against eavesdropping, but when it involves Isa getting the hell out of Waterside?

Yes. Please. More.

"You can't quit," Rico says. His voice sounds weird, like he's having trouble talking for some reason. "I won't let you."

"Yes, I can. My great-aunt's starting a new restaurant near downtown that'll kick Waterside's pathetic ass. You'll be out of business in no time."

Holy shit. Isa wants to put Waterside out of business? She's shadier than I thought. No one is allowed to do that. Waterside is like . . . a haven for teenagers or something. Or at least it was, before Rico took over and started ruining stuff.

Rico pauses, and I hear Isa's shoes squeak, like she's turning to go. "You don't want to do that," he says finally.

"And why the hell not?" she asks. Her voice is like rattlesnake venom.

Damn. I've only ever heard her that mad once, and that was when Elaine slapped her.

"Because I'll tell a certain doctor that you swiped his keys and broke into his house."

My eyes widen. Peter looks up from wiping down the kitchen. He glances at me and puts a finger to his lips, his eyes wide.

"That's bullshit," Isa spits. "I didn't break into anyone's house and you know it."

"Well, that's really weird, Isa, because his house was broken into last night. And you just happen to have keys. What did you think, that everyone was going to keep your dirty little secret just because of Tips? You quit this job, or you let your aunt open that restaurant, and you're going to jail, sweetheart."

"You think you can blackmail me?" Isa shouts.

"You're a criminal," Rico says. "Think about it. Where'd you get all that extra cash if you didn't steal shit to get it?"

Extra cash? Shit. He has to be talking about the money I'm giving her. Which means I could be in trouble too, if the cops start asking about *that*. I step back from the door and hide between the refrigerators just before Rico stalks out of his office. Isa comes out a few moments later, and I come out from my hiding spot. Her eyes are red and angry.

"I need to talk to you," I say. "Really bad."

"Screw you, Finn."

I hold up my hands. "I know you didn't do it, Isa. And I'm going to help you."

She stares at me, her mouth open in a small O shape. "Why?" she finally asks.

It's a good question. It's not like we're exactly on great terms.

"Let's get into your car and talk," I say.

"But we're not off," she points out.

I stare at her. "Do you really care right now? Let Rico take care of it."

She looks down at the floor. "Okay," she says. "Let's go."

I follow her out to her car. Her hands shake as she puts the key in the ignition.

"You heard that, huh?" she asks. The car whines to life.

"Yeah," I say. "Isa . . . how did Rico find out about your extra cash?"

Isa's lips tighten. "I don't know. I hid it in my car. Maybe he saw you give it to me."

"He wasn't there."

"I don't know how he knows, okay, Finn? He just *does*. Isn't that what being an adult is all about? Knowing shit you have no business knowing?"

I don't respond. She puts her car in drive and we leave the back lot. Gravel pops and cracks under the tires. We drive along the shoreline for a long time. The night is deceivingly peaceful. Too calm for good things.

"So," she says eventually. "I guess life is over." She hasn't cried one drop, but her eyes are wet with held-in tears.

"No," I say. "It's really not."

Isa laughs, and the sound catches strangely in her throat. Her hands shake on her steering wheel.

"I'm going to help you. You do some shady stuff, Isa, but I don't think you would break into someone's house and steal their shit. Now, you might blackmail someone else to do it . . ." I trail off.

She laughs again, but the sound is thick with pain. "Why are you being nice to me, Finn?"

I shrug. "I'm not doing it to be nice. I want to make a deal with you." I roll down my window, just slightly, to let in a whisper of night air.

"Sure. A deal." Her voice is empty. She slows the car and rolls over to the side of the road, and she looks at me, slow and intense.

"I help you get out of this . . . and I quit my side job. Forever. No more money."

Isa thinks about it for a long time. Her short fingers tap on her armrest.

"But—"

"And if you try to tell, if you whisper a word of it"—I pause and lean forward to pull a crumpled bit of newspaper out of my back pocket—"this might get passed around. You were a beauty queen, huh?"

"Where did you get that?" Isa hisses, and snatches at the article.

I pull it back, out of her reach. "Nowhere." I fold it neatly and slide it back into my pocket. "But if you go back on your word, if you tell a soul about my business, then all of your new friends at Waterside will see this."

Isa takes her eyes off the road to glare at me. "You're an ass," she says. "I'm in a crisis here and you're bringing up this petty shit?"

"Take it or leave it." I won't let myself feel bad. I won't.

"Okay," she agrees finally. "It's a deal."

Xavi
Tuesday

The four-wheeler hits the ravine hard and I almost bounce off the seat. Shifting my grip, I hold onto the handlebars as tight as I can, and the wheels find purchase on the dirt and I climb up out of the ravine. Part of me wants to drive over to the shed, but Peter might be there. He loves that old, falling-apart building. And, if I'm being honest, so do I. But I need to be alone right now. I need to figure my life out before it's too late.

Ha. Who am I kidding?

It's already too late.

I drive along the opposite side of the pasture, very slowly, and peer over toward my neighbor's property. The engine of the four-wheeler purrs. Our neighbor, Chasey Waters, who lives just to the south of us, owns a jungle. Well, it's not really a jungle. It's more of a junkyard, but I used to call it "the jungle" when I was little. Back then, my mother was married to this guy called Ellis, and I had a brother named Nick. Nick and I would walk out here to the junkyard, with a picnic of that weird cheese in a can and Ritz crackers in tow, and we'd climb all over the old stuff. We'd play king of the castle.

Then one day Nick tripped over a half-buried paint can and gashed his forehead on a license plate. He had to get a tetanus shot and twelve stitches and we weren't allowed back to the jungle anymore.

I slow down near the edge, where an old red tractor is half poking out of an overgrown evergreen, and park the four-wheeler near the trees. Chasey never found us playing in the junkyard before, or maybe he just pretended he couldn't see us when we hid, but I'm not going to take any crazy chances now.

I stomp through my old playground. I wish I could go back to those days. Even just one. I wish I could grab the little girl that I was and whisper some advice in her ear: "Don't sleep with your stepbrother on the floor of a bar. Or, like, anywhere."

That would probably teach me.

I might even add something about not taking naked pictures for your boss, if I wanted to provide a real learning moment.

More than likely, though, I'd scare my stupid younger self doing my Christmas Carol thing and then—*bam*, early-onset heart attack. Future—gone. But at least then I'd never get knocked up.

The junkyard hasn't changed much. At least, not the part we played in. It has grown, though, so large that it nearly reaches Chasey's home. It's a surprisingly swank house, especially to be right next to a pile of junk. It's all mod, so my mom hates it and says it's like the worst eyesore of all eyesores, but I think it's cool.

I hear the growl of a car engine and jump behind the old rusted-out frame of a Ford. I don't want Chasey to catch me sneaking around. I press my back to the old car door and raise myself up slowly. I peer through the broken-out window of the Ford. That weird Audi hatchback looks suspiciously like one of Rico's cars, but the dude has, like, eight, so I can't be sure.

Chasey walks up to the vehicle. He's wearing overalls with one strap tossed casually over his shoulder. Totally embracing hillbilly culture. I have to give him cred for his counter-fab style.

The door of the Audi swings open, and Rico steps out.

Weird with more weirdness. I wouldn't think Rico would be caught dead talking to someone like Chasey. Rico pretends to be all class and style and general sleaze, and that does not include fraternizing with people who may or may not be named Billy Bob.

Rico clicks a button on his keyless entry, and the hatchback rises. He messes around inside of it for a minute and comes out with a gigantic speaker. The nice kind.

My skin goes all prickly. Something's off.

Chasey takes the speaker and sits it on the hood of an old Impala. "How many of these you got?" he asks.

I duck and move over one truck, slowly and quietly, so I can peer into the back of Rico's car.

Holy shit.

There's, like, four more speakers in there.

Rico motions at them. "And three more at home. Think you could sell them somewhere?"

Chasey rests his chin between his thumb and forefinger. "These look nice. I reckon I could unload them. Where'd you get them?"

Rico hunches his shoulders. "Uh, just picked 'em up from a friend."

Holy shit. Do I or do I not remember hearing that Dr. Li had tons of stereo equipment stolen from his house?

Did *Rico* break into Dr. Li's house?

But why would Rico do that? He owns a swank restaurant that's doing pretty well. Why would he risk it all to lift some speakers?

I think of the unpaid bills on his desk.

By the looks of that—and his extravagant lifestyle—he needs the cash.

"Why don't we unload the rest of these and we can do some paperwork inside?" Chasey asks. He motions at his house, but Rico's already shaking his head.

"No paperwork," Rico says suddenly. "None at all."

Chasey spits on the ground next to Rico's feet. "My fee's a lot higher if this is a paperwork-free deal, young man."

Rico shrugs. "It is what it is, you know?" He reaches into the hatchback and comes out with another speaker, larger than the first. "Help me unload these."

Very, very slowly, I pull my cell phone from my pocket and raise it up above the bed of the pickup truck. And I snap a picture of Rico with the huge speaker in his arms.

It's clear. And I can clearly see the brand—or at least, a big *I* under his hand.

I watch them unload the rest of the hatchback.

"Hey," Rico says. "Do you think you could find a place for some nice art?"

Chasey scratches his head. "Original stuff?"

Rico nods.

Chasey spits again. "You're out of luck. That's too easy to track, son. I won't have nothing to do with it."

I clap my hand over my mouth.

Chasey freezes.

"What?" Rico asks.

I duck down, my back to the pickup truck. Shit.

"Just thought I heard something."

Both of them are silent, and I stay still. Crap. Did they hear me? Are they going to find me crouched here?

"Probably a squirrel or something," Chasey mutters. "Anyway. No art. I won't say more about it."

Was art missing from Dr. Li's house? I don't remember. But why else would Rico want to get rid of art? And if it wasn't stolen, why wouldn't Chasey want it? I mean, it sounds valuable. Probably.

I send the picture to Peter and wait, making myself very quiet and small while Rico and Chasey finish talking. Finally Rico climbs back into his hatchback and drives away, leaving a thick cloud of dust in his wake.

I sink down to the dirt on the opposite side of the truck, giving Chasey the opportunity to get back to his house with the speakers.

My boss, Rico, was the one who broke into the house.

Not Isa.

Not anyone else.

Fucking *Rico*.

This whole thing has gone wrong. More than wrong.

And suddenly I'm smack-dab in the middle of it.

Peter
Tuesday

Xavi bursts into my room, her cell phone clutched tight in her hand. She looks winded, and her normally smooth hair looks like she's just walked through a tornado. She's wearing these itty-bitty jean shorts, and her tank top is pulled up so I can see part of her still-smooth stomach.

It's sort of hot.

"Peter, oh my damn, Peter, did you get it? You have to help me. You got it, right?" She starts pacing back and forth beside my bed. "What are we supposed to do? I mean, I saw it—what am I supposed to do? And I sent it to you, and now you're involved . . ."

She falls back onto my bed, puts her face in her hands, and makes this weird squally sound that only girls can pull off.

What the hell is she talking about? I didn't get anything from her. Actually, I'd been sort of looking at a magazine. Of sorts. I stay carefully seated.

"What?" I ask.

"Look at your cell phone, Peter!" She jumps off the bed, exasperated.

I pick it up and unlock it. Two new messages: one from

Finn, about telling Rico he'd be late or something, and one from Xavi. An image.

I open it and see Rico. Rico, holding what looks to be a very expensive piece of stereo equipment in the middle of some junkyard. His Audi visible in the background, and the whole back looks totally full of badass stereo equipment. The legit stuff too—the stuff that I'd asked my dad about last year. He told me I could get it if Dale Earnhardt came back from the grave and returned to NASCAR to slap his punk son in the face.

Aka no.

"Xavi," I say. "What is this?"

"I was four-wheeling in the pastures, and I went by Chasey's place because I felt like walking through the jungle—the junkyard—and they were just there. Making some sort of shady deal. It was totally like a scene from *The Godfather*."

"Slow down, okay?" I hold up my hands. "Are you thinking what I'm thinking?"

She nods very deliberately. "And he said something about not wanting paperwork and getting rid of paintings or whatever."

"Hold up." I swivel around in my chair to face my laptop and pull up the local newspaper. Dr. Li's robbery is still front-page news, so I click on the article. Xavi leans over my shoulder to read along with me.

"Look," I say, my finger following the line on the screen. "Stolen from the residence was a high-end stereo system, jewelry, and rare art . . . holy shit. There was art, too. And cash, maybe. It looks like a safe was broken into." He scrolls down the page.

Xavi fidgets. She smells wonderful—all fresh and sweet from the outdoors, and for a half second I want to push aside all the Rico bullshit and kiss her. But now is not the time.

She tangles her fingers in her hair. "I mean, I didn't see it, but he asked Chasey about it. And Chasey said he didn't deal with original art because it was easy to track." She pauses. "I don't want to get Chasey in trouble, Peter."

"I get that." Chasey's been her neighbor her whole life. "Maybe he won't. You didn't get him in the picture."

"But it's clearly his land," she points out. "Who else has that much crap?"

I sigh. "It's Chasey or Isa. And Isa didn't do anything wrong. She was working last night."

"Besides steal Dr. Li's keys in the first place. But yeah, I highly doubt she actually stole anything else. Isa isn't exactly the Shining Example of Perfect Morals, but Rico's way more likely to break into someone's house. I mean, the pictures." Xavi sits down on the edge of the desk. "And if Isa gets in trouble, well, maybe Finn will get in trouble. Maybe we'll all get in trouble. It was our money that funded everything. We're accomplices."

"So is Rico using Tips to frame Isa for the crime?"

"Looks like it. Oh my damn, oh my *damn*. Peter, this is totally insane."

I look at her. She's beautiful. "I know, Xav."

Xavi gives me sort of a weak half smile, and I reach out and take her hand. She doesn't pull away.

"So what do we do?"

I look at the picture. Rico . . . What a fucking scum of the earth asswipe. I think of what he did to Xavi, of what he did to all of those girls, and a white-hot rage starts under my skin. I want to beat the shit out of him all over again.

"I think," I say carefully, "if you're cool with it, we need to call Isa."

Xavi interlaces her fingers with mine. "I don't know. Should we tell our parents?"

I shake my head. There's too much going on to tell them right now. I don't want them to find out about Xavi's other problem. Not yet. Not until she's ready. "Let's just sit tight, okay?" I reach out to touch her hair with my other hand, but I draw back, unsure.

Xavi bites her bottom lip. "Peter?"

"Yeah?"

"Do you like Rico?"

I feel my lip pull up. "The dude is the antichrist. I can't stand him." My hand tightens on Xavi's.

Xavi picks up a little *Doctor Who* action figure from my desk. "I thought you sort of liked him. That you were buds or whatever. And I heard that he's only being weird about money because he's paying for his dad to be in a rest home."

Huh. I didn't know that. But that doesn't excuse what he did to Xavi. I can't forgive him for that. Ever.

"Yeah, well, I used to get along with him. But then I found out about what he was asking some girls at work to do. I got rid of the pictures, but I can't fucking *stand* him. And no matter what he's spending his money on, he deserves to be in prison."

Xavi's cheeks color. "Those girls are stupid, Peter." She drops the figurine back on my desk.

I look up at her, and her eyes flicker to mine. "Maybe they

had a less-than-proud moment or something. Maybe they screwed up. But they were still taken advantage of by someone in a position of power. That's wrong, Xavi."

She looks at me for a long second and squeezes my hand. "Yeah. Maybe."

We sit there for a minute, just together. I want to ask her how she's feeling. If she's still feeling . . . sick.

"Hey, Peter?" Xavi says finally, interrupting my thoughts.

"Yeah?"

"I think we need to call Isa."

"You have her number?"

She picks up her cell phone and hands it to me, and I scroll through her contacts to *Isa Sanchez*. I hit dial, and the phone rings three times.

"Hello?"

I look at Xavi, and for some reason, her eyes have this nervous fluttering thing going on.

"Hey, Isa. It's Peter. Listen . . . Xavi found out something I think you're going to want to know."

Isa hesitates. "I work today. Do you want to meet me at the restaurant in twenty?"

"Is Rico there?"

"Finn said he's not coming in until later tonight."

Hmm. Finn and Isa are speaking again. Weird.

"Perfect. Xavi and I will be there. See you soon."

Isa
Tuesday

I pound my fists on the countertop. The pans rattle.

"That asshole," Finn breathes beside me. "What kind of person *does* that?"

Xavi, Finn, Peter, and I are standing around the countertop in the kitchen. Warren's taking the tables, and we made an executive decision to make Jake a waiter for the day. Probably not the best idea, but whatever. We needed to get him out of the kitchens, and Warren needed help on the floor. Plus I don't exactly care about Rico's perfect business anymore.

I look back down at the phone and Rico, hanging on to the speaker or subwoofer or whatever it is. Rico, with Dr. Li's stolen property, which he tried to pass off on *me*. He was going to ruin my entire life.

The rage in my chest physically hurts. I want to feed this asshole through a wood chipper. He messed with the wrong girl.

"He took the keys from my car," I say. "He must have gotten *my* keys out of my purse. That's how he knew about my money. It was with Dr. Li's keys."

"What money?" Peter asks. He leans back against the fridge, one leg crossed casually over the other.

Ugh. I should never have mentioned the money. Peter's too smart. I look down at my hands.

"Money I lent her," Finn says. "Isa was having a little . . . trouble, so I loaned her some. She's going to pay it back—right, Isa?" He nudges me. He looks painfully different today in his board shorts and gray T-shirt. Nothing like the starched, elegant Finn we're all used to.

I glare at him. No. "Of course, Finn."

"Then why not take that money?" Xavi leans forward onto her elbows and puts her cheek in her hand. "Much easier than breaking into some rich dude's house."

"Then what would he frame Isa with?" Finn asks. "And he got way more out of Li's house than what I gave Isa."

Whoa. Finn actually sounds sort of smart.

"So what do I do?" Isa asks. "I can't let him do this to me."

"Obviously." Xavi rolls her eyes. "Rico's the biggest tool in the belt. I want to see him gone. Even if it means Waterside goes too."

Everyone's quiet for a second. Waterside. Gone. It's hard to swallow.

Peter clears his throat. "Yeah. He needs to go. I say we hang the frame back where it's supposed to be."

Xavi frowns at him. "Seriously, Peter? I don't even know what that means. You are such a dork." She pushes him sort of playfully, and he looks at her in this weird way, like he wants to bite her.

Stepsiblings are so strange.

"So what do you propose?" I ask.

"Well," Peter says slowly. "We know he sold those speakers to Chasey, right? And we have proof. So there's step one in going to the cops. And we happen to have keys, don't we?" He looks at me.

"We happen to have keys."

Finn checks his cell phone. "Rico will be here in about an hour. Maybe less. What can we do in an hour?"

Peter grins and ducks down to rummage under the sink. He comes back up with a red screwdriver. "Isa?" he says.

"Yeah?"

He arches an eyebrow at me. "I think we put the keys back where they should be."

"With Dr. Li?" I ask. "No way. He'll think I did it."

He presses his thumb to his chin. "Nope. With the guy who actually broke into Dr. Li's house."

We all turn and look toward Rico's office. The door is closed, but it isn't locked. It's never locked.

"Oh," I breathe. "Right."

"Get to work," says Peter. He flips the screwdriver and holds it out to me, handle first.

As I take it, I feel a smile creep over my face. Rico thinks he's all smart and shit, but he doesn't know who he's messing with.

We all go into Rico's office, and I kneel down by his air-conditioning vent. The screws come off easily—like they have a hundred times before. There's paperwork in the vent, taped to the bottom and the sides. God knows what that is. I hope it's something illegal.

I go back into the staff bathroom and untape the keys, still wrapped tightly in the napkin, from above the ceiling tile. If Rico was the last one to touch them, then his prints should be on the keys. He must have rewrapped them when he finished with Dr. Li's house.

I put them carefully on the lip of the air-conditioning vent.

"Don't screw it on too tight," Xavi says from behind me.

"Why?" I ask.

"It shouldn't look right," she says, tilting her head. "Make it obvious."

"Of course." I leave the screw at the bottom right-hand corner halfway out. Someone could remove it with a hand—a couple of twists and it'd be out. I tighten the rest a little more, but not too much.

Behind me, Xavi is dialing Rico's phone. "Yes, I'd like to provide information on a crime. Can you meet me? Waterside Café? Right. See you soon."

She hangs up and crosses her arms over her chest. "They'll be here in twenty minutes. And they might want to check out my new background."

She shows me her phone. Rico, with the speakers in his arms, is her display. I laugh. "Xavi?" I say.

"Hmm?" She slips her phone into her pocket. She's not working tonight, so she's wearing jeans and a loose-fitting tank.

"Thanks."

"It's the right thing to do, isn't it?" she asks. "Come on. Back to the kitchen. We're having guests."

Peter's laying out fluffy little choux pastry puffs in neat circles on a papered tray, like nothing is happening. Warren comes back. "For the customers?" he asks, reaching for a puff, but Finn grabs the tray out of his reach.

"No. They have the crème brûlée today. The pastries are for employees only."

Warren takes one and pops it whole into his mouth. He groans. "Peter, dude. I think I just fell in love with you and I don't care who knows it." He turns and stalks back out to the floor, wiping his fingers on his cummerbund and leaving faint little sugary smudges. Rico would so not approve.

Peter laughs and replaces the little carameled cream puff with another just like it. "Isa?" he asks. "Take one?"

My stomach is too nervous. I wrap my hands around myself, trying to be still. "No thanks. Maybe after?"

"After," Peter warns, "they might be gone."

I try to laugh. Like food is my biggest concern right now. "I'll risk it."

Before he can say anything else there's a loud knock at the back door. My heart does a strange, violent tremor in my chest.

This is it.

Xavi rushes over and swings the door open.

Two uniformed police officers—one I think I recognize as the sheriff—walk in. The screen door creaks noisily shut behind them. They look around, taking in the kitchen, and focus in on Xavi—who suddenly looks very small and very young, standing there alone.

"Are you Xavi Mitchell?" the taller one asks. His brown eyes flick to Peter, and to me for a moment, and my skin feels like stone. I couldn't move if I wanted to.

This could be the end of my life right now if they know I took those keys.

"Yes, sir." Her hands find the hem of her tank top, and she pulls at it. "We—ah—we need to talk. I think I know exactly who broke into Dr. Li's home." She unlocks her phone and holds it out so they can see the picture. "That's my boss. I'm sure you've heard of him."

The cops exchange glances. Of course they have.

"And how did you gain possession of this photo?" the short one—the sheriff—asks. He has weird green eyes and red hair, and he looks about as funny as a funeral. This dude means business.

But Xavi, to her credit, doesn't flinch.

"I was on the edge of my family's property, where it meets my neighbor's land. I saw my boss trying to sell my neighbor speakers, and he said he didn't want paperwork. And he talked about original art, too. And I looked on the Internet and it said art and a stereo system were stolen. You can check the photo. It's from today. I think there's a time stamp and everything."

I have to hand it to Xavi. She doesn't even sound nervous. She sounds like she's relating gossip to her BFF or something.

"Your neighbor is who?" asks the tall cop.

Finally Xavi flinches, and her shoulders tense up to her ears. "Chasey. Chasey Miller."

The taller cop takes the phone, and he exchanges a look with the sheriff. "Miss Mitchell, I'm Detective Martin Wilder, and this is Sheriff Malcolm Heathers. We have a warrant to search the premises." He shows Xavi a piece of paper. "Why don't you show us to your boss's office?"

My heart beats through my chest. Holy *shit*. They already have a warrant? A freaking *warrant*? Did this mean they had other reasons to suspect Rico?

Or did they suspect me?

I feel a hot blush creeping up my neck to my face. Be cool, Isa. Please. Be cool. My hands get sweaty and strange.

Xavi takes the officers into Rico's little office and closes the door.

I want to press my ear to the door. I want to be in there with them. But Xavi's the witness. They need to talk to her alone.

"Um," I say to Peter. "Can I help?"

He shrugs. "Sure. Can you cook?"

I shake my head. I'm not good at it. My great-aunt, though—she's awesome. Absolutely fantastic. But since we're saving money, dinner usually consists of little boxed meals from the frozen-food section at Walmart. Minimally nutritious or delicious.

I look back at Rico's office.

I need to know what's going on in there.

"Do me a favor. Just *try* the pastries. I'm testing them out for next week's menu." He puts one on a saucer and pushes it at me. I take a tentative bite, and I don't taste it at all. I'm vaguely aware of a sticky sweetness, but for all I can tell, I'm eating dried-up paint.

"What do you think?" Peter asks. I know he's being nice and trying to calm me down when the cops are here. I wonder, absurdly, if I should have tried for a date with Peter instead of Finn.

I swallow the rest of the puff. "It's amazing." The lie comes easily, and my eyes are still stuck to the door of the office.

Finn reaches over me to grab one off the tray. "Great, man," he says. "Did Dubois send you the recipe for these?"

"Uh," Peter says, "no. I sort of figured them out myself. But Dubois hasn't updated the menu lately, and people are asking for new stuff. I thought—"

"You're not supposed to be updating the menu, Peter," Rico says. "We talked about this. This is Chef Dubois's menu.

Not some high school kid's Fisher Price Guide to French Cuisine."

I flip around. And there he is.

Standing right behind me.

Too close.

Way too close.

He smells like he doused himself in aftershave and his face looks like he lost a battle with Mike Tyson. "Who's in my office, Isa?" he asks.

There's a thin line of light coming out from beneath the door.

I lock eyes with him. "Who do you think is in there, Rico?"

He glares at me and stalks off to his office. "Finn," he says, "what the hell are you doing here? You're not even scheduled to work."

Finn ignores him, like Rico isn't even there. He grabs another puff and winks at me.

Rico pulls at the handle of the door.

It's locked.

He looks back at us, his lip curled up. "What's going on?" he asks.

Peter shrugs cheerfully. "Figure it out."

Rico balls up his fist and pounds on the door. "Who the fuck is in there?" he says, his voice strained. "Get out. *Now.*"

Finn
Tuesday

A cop opens the door. The one named Heathers, I think.

And Rico just stares.

His mouth opens slightly, and then closes, and opens again. Like a goldfish.

"The hell are you doing in my office?" he says slowly, but his voice loses volume like a balloon deflating.

Detective Wilder walks behind Sheriff Heathers, and I hear his shoe connect with something hard and metal, which clatters to the floor, followed by the jangle of—

Keys.

Dr. Li's keys.

Isa grabs onto my arm. "The air-conditioning vent," she whispers. "It worked. It fucking worked."

"That's what we're doing," says Detective Wilder.

Sheriff Heathers crosses his arms over his broad chest. "Are you familiar with your Miranda rights, Rico Harris?"

Rico stands there, stupefied. "This is my restaurant," he says. His arms motion wildly around him. "It's mine."

"Yes," Sheriff Heathers replies. "And this is your arrest." He pulls the handcuffs out of his back pocket, and Rico turns away and takes off running, his expensive black shoes squeaking on the floor.

I'm not the quarterback for one of the best football teams in the state just because my daddy's the head coach.

I race after him, my arms out. He slams through the double doors and sprints out past the first row of tables.

I tear through the doors, and one hits me in the shoulder as it swings closed. Rico bumps into tables, rattling water glasses. Warren freezes, a plate halfway to the table, his jaw slightly open.

And then Rico catches his shoe on the leg of a table.

He doesn't fall, but he stumbles.

It's all I need to catch up.

I grab him around the middle and tackle him, hard, to the floor. His hand closes on a tablecloth, and he brings it all down on top of us—glasses, silverware, and the night's menu. He struggles, and I push him down, holding his shoulders to the floor.

The cops sprint in after us. Detective Wilder draws his gun from the holster on his hip and aims it at Rico.

"You have the right to remain silent," he begins, the barrel pointing steadily at Rico while Heathers moves forward with the cuffs in his hands. "Anything you say can and will be used against you in a court of law."

Rico throws his arm over into the mess of the fallen tablecloth. His hand closes around a fork that has come loose from a napkin. He grips it tightly, and in one quick, violent arc—

He stabs me in the back.

I grunt as I feel the metal spokes pierce my skin. Reaching up, I grab his hand and force it back to the ground, and then the pain starts, a sharp, thick bolt of it, near my spine.

Rico tries to slam me with his forehead, but I raise up, out of his reach, and put a knee in his groin. "Don't fucking move," I growl.

He glares hate at me.

Sheriff Heathers lands on one side of me and pins Rico down, while Detective Wilder grabs his other wrist, twisting cruelly.

"We got 'em, Finn," Heathers grunts.

I stand up slowly, wincing.

"Oh my damn, Finn!" Xavi comes running from the kitchen. "Should we call an ambulance? It's, like, sticking out of you! Did it hit any vital organs?"

I groan. I don't think so, but it hurts like a bitch.

Rico screams on the ground, writhing under the weight of Sheriff Heathers, who has his knee in Rico's back and Rico's hands cuffed together. His face is smashed into the fancy tile by Detective Wilder's shoe, but he's still screeching.

"That bitch did it!" he shouts, his voice cracking. "That bitch Isa Sanchez! It was a dare! It was Tips! She stole everything!"

Detective Wilder blinks at him. "Let's get him to the station," he says, and Heathers hoists Rico up by the arms. He looks at me. "We'll get some medics here to look at that, and then we'll need you down at the station for a statement. You too," he says, nodding at Xavi. "You'll both need to call your parents right now."

"Yes, sir." I try to start forward, but the pain in my back stops me. I grit my teeth and touch my finger to the fork, which is still *in* there, and starting to weep hot blood.

Detective Wilder hesitates for a minute, then says, "I used to play too. Tips." He grins. "Off the record, of course."

He winks at Isa, who is standing behind us, her arms crossed over her chest. "So . . ."

"So I'd say your Tips days are over, but I get it." He puts on a pair of shades. "Be careful, okay?"

He walks out with Rico in tow, and Isa smiles rather wickedly. And then she laughs. She laughs until she's bent over.

"What?" I ask, wincing at the pain.

She straightens, and there are tears running down her red cheeks.

"You know," she says, "my great-aunt's opening up a new restaurant next summer. So, if you all want to keep Tips going?"

"Isa?" I say. "No thanks."

Xavi
Tuesday

Ambulances and cop cars.

It's been a hell of a day.

Finn's sitting in the back of the ambulance while they put a butterfly bandage on his wound. His dad is going to be super pissed. He'll be out of practice for a little while to heal, but at least he'll be back in time for the season. And he'll always have a weird-ass fork scar to remember Rico by.

Peter comes up behind me and slides his arms around my waist. He presses his warm lips against my neck. "Do you need a ride to the station?" he asks. "I called your mom. She's going to meet you."

I could probably drive myself, but I want him there. I want Peter with me. I turn around and wrap my arms around him. "Would you?"

He looks into my eyes. "Anything, okay? Anything you need. Anything you want. From here on out."

"Really?" I ask. I know he means more than just a ride to the police station.

His hand brushes my stomach.

He's talking about the baby.

He nods. "I'm here for you, Xavi." He touches my cheek.

He means it. Peter—sweet, dorky, infinitely cool Peter—means it.

I pause. "Then I have something to tell you, Peter."

He swallows hard. "Okay."

"Would you still want to be with me if I wasn't pregnant?" I ask. "Are you, like feeling a sense of duty or something?" I don't meet his eyes. I study the pocket of his shirt instead. I can feel his heart beating against me.

He lifts my chin up with a finger and looks at me intently. "Are you saying what I think you're saying?"

I grin. I can't help it. "I—um—got my period. I didn't say anything because it was right before the cops got here. But I'm not pregnant. It must've just been the stomach flu, like I first thought."

Peter picks me up in his arms and spins me in a circle until I'm giggling. "Are you serious?"

I nod.

He takes my face in his hands and kisses me. "Xavi. Shit. I am so happy. I love you."

I bury my face in his neck. "I'm really, really glad I'm not having your baby."

He laughs. "Me too."

I snuggle against him. "Hey."

He brushes my hair back and touches my bottom lip. "Yeah?"

"Would you be mad if maybe we slowed things down a little? I mean . . . physically?"

He pulls away from me so he can see my eyes. "Xavi. Anything you want. Whatever you're ready for or not ready for. Okay?"

I nod. "Okay."

He holds me for a long time. The boy I thought I hated and turned out to love. This is some serious Jane Austen shit right here.

I smile into his shirt. "I love you, too," I whisper, just loud enough for him to hear.

Life is a funny thing.

Isa
Tuesday

Did Xavi and Peter just make out in front of everybody?
It's like your boss gets arrested and your friend gets stabbed
with a fork and suddenly just everything is okay.

Ew.

Acknowledgments

First and foremost, I'd like to thank my mom and dad, Steve and Kate Morgan, who believed in me more than I ever thought to believe in myself. It's a powerful thing, even if you don't realize it. For Lindsay and Ryan, who were always there.

I'd like to thank the professors and teachers who slipped me extra books and good advice. To Lexi Larsen, David Colby, and Tammy Gibson for being invaluable sets of eyes for early pages.

A huge, resounding thank-you to Suzanne Young and Bethany Griffin, who are the best readers and writers and friends anyone could ask for. And to the musers, who were with me every step of the way.

Thanks to Michael Strother, a most amazing editor. You deserve a billion cupcakes!